AMISH INN MYSTERIES™

The Hound *and the* Fury

Sandra Orchard

Annie's®

AnniesFiction.com

Library of Congress-in-Publication Data
The Hound and the Fury / by Sandra Orchard
p. cm.
I. Title
                    2017950980

AnniesFiction.com
(800) 282-6643
Amish Inn Mysteries™
Series Creator: Shari Lohner
Series Editor: Jane Haertel
Cover Illustrator: Kelley McMorris

10 11 12 13 14 | Printed in China | 9 8 7 6 5 4 3 2 1

1

"Did you know evergreens represent hope in adversity?" Amy Cooper asked as her friend Liz Eckardt hacked off another spruce branch from a tree in the side yard of the Olde Mansion Inn.

"I didn't know that." Liz added the new branch to the bundle her friend held. "I just like how nice they make the inn smell."

A tan sedan turned into the driveway, with a little dog in the passenger seat, barking excitedly.

"That'll be one of my guests," Liz said. "We'd better head in."

"I can finish laying these around the fireplace mantels while you check them in," Amy said and headed around to the back of the inn.

Liz caught up to her tall, brown-eyed guest and his adorable beagle on the front porch. "You must be John Baxter."

"That's right." The cleft in his chin deepened when he smiled.

"Welcome to the Olde Mansion Inn. I'm the owner, Liz Eckardt."

He started to extend his hand but stopped short, eyeing the Amish corn knife she'd been using to cut branches.

She switched the hook-shaped blade to her left hand. "I was cutting greenery for Christmas decorations," she explained, meeting his handshake.

He grinned. "Got to love that smell."

Liz returned his smile. It was nice to know her guests would appreciate her efforts. "Follow me and I'll get you checked in." She escorted him to the reception desk and set the corn knife on the table behind her before logging into the computer to pull up his registration.

He handed her a stack of crisp bills to pay for the three nights he'd booked.

She turned the guest book toward him to fill in. "You're here for the dog competition?"

"Yup, the tracking trial is this afternoon. It's all in the nose." He affectionately rubbed the scruff of his dog's neck. "Peanut here can track just about anything." John slid the book back across the desk to Liz. "Will you be there?"

Liz held out her hand for her four-legged guest to smell. "I should, to cheer you on, right, Peanut?"

The dog woofed, tail wagging.

Amy, coming in from the dining room, laughed. "I guess that settles it." She turned her dazzling smile on John. "Hi, I'm Amy Cooper, visiting from Boston. I've never been to a dog competition before, and I don't think Liz has either. Perhaps you could give us an inside scoop on the must-sees?" Her tone had a flirtatious lilt that sent a twinge of surprise down Liz's spine.

Liz returned her attention to the computer screen. John's affection for his dog was sweet, and she couldn't blame Amy for flirting.

Liz never flirted with guests. Or with anyone for that matter.

Then again, in all the years she'd known Amy, neither had she. Not through all their years as friends during college and law school, and certainly not with the eighty-hour work weeks that followed, as Amy tried to make partner at her Boston law firm and Liz juggled work and raising her orphaned godson, Steve.

Two more guests and their perfectly coiffed miniature poodles arrived. John and Amy stepped out of their path and proceeded to chat as if they were old friends.

Amy's easy conversation with John was as out of character as her showing up at the inn out of the blue the day before, announcing she'd decided it was time for a vacation in Indiana—at Liz's inn—in the first week of December. Since all of the rooms in the inn were reserved,

Liz had put up Amy in her own quarters, where she slept on the sofa in Liz's small sitting room.

Not that Liz didn't think Pleasant Creek was a beautiful place, but if *she* were still part of the rat race in Boston, she was pretty sure somewhere tropical would have been higher on her list of preferred destinations.

Liz handed the poodle owners, Tiffany and Tara, keys to the Sunrise and Sunset Rooms on the top floor of the inn. "I hope you enjoy your stay. And feel free to join us for light refreshments in the sitting room later this afternoon."

As the pair synchronized their watches with the grandfather clock in the hall, John also glanced at the time. "I'm afraid I have to run." He picked up his suitcase and smiled at Amy. "See you at the show?"

"Absolutely. Sounds like fun."

His smile, which looked like it belonged in a toothpaste commercial, would've made any girl's knees go weak.

It made Amy giggle. She watched John climb the inn's staircase to his second-floor room then turned to Liz. "I'm beginning to see why this place has managed to keep you away from the city so long."

Liz studied her friend curiously. "Since when do you take time to date?"

"Hey, life's too short to let opportunities slip away. So what do you say? Can you spare a couple of hours to watch the dog show with me this afternoon?"

"Sure. If that's what you want to do." Liz had been eager to check out Pleasant Creek's latest event anyway. She could thank the three-day dog show for nicely filling the inn with both two- and four-legged guests. "Sarah can keep an eye on things while I'm gone." Sarah Borkholder was a young Amish woman who worked part-time at the inn, managing to keep it cleaner than Liz could have even if she'd devoted all her time to the task.

"Where are you off to?" Mary Ann Berne asked from the doorway of Sew Welcome, the fabric shop that opened off the inn's rotunda. She walked over to Liz and Amy at the desk.

"Tracking trials!" Amy exclaimed. "Would you like to join us?"

"Ooh," squealed Sadie Schwarzentruber, who co-owned the shop with Mary Ann. Sadie stepped up next to Mary Ann with a stack of quilting squares in her hand

"What a brilliant idea! Beans will be a shoo-in."

"*No*," Liz said firmly. "We're just going to watch." The overweight English bulldog who had come with the inn had an occasional talent for finding things—when he wasn't sleeping—but they were usually things that entangled Liz in a heap of trouble. And she'd had enough of that to last a lifetime. "We're going to cheer for my *guests'* dogs."

"I'm game to join you," Sadie said. "We can swing by my house so I can grab my camera. What do you say, Mary Ann?"

"Well, we've been pretty slow all morning. I suppose there's no harm in closing the shop for a couple of hours," Mary Ann conceded.

Sadie turned to Liz. "I still think you should enter Beans. He is a purebred, you know."

Beans lay on his favorite rug near the front door, an infinitesimal twitch of his ears the only indication he'd heard the suggestion.

Sadie walked over to him. "Wouldn't you like that, Beans?" she cooed.

He quirked open one eye, let out a long, lazy yawn, then buried his face under his paw.

Mary Ann chuckled. "Guess that settles that."

Sadie shot him a disappointed frown then grabbed her keys from her purse. "I'll drive."

"We can get a snack at Sweet Everything before we leave, and see if Naomi wants to join us too," Mary Ann suggested. "Naomi makes the best cupcakes in town, and her bakery is right next door," she explained to Amy. "She's also a member of our quilting group. If Liz didn't already tell you, we call ourselves the Material Girls."

"How fun." Amy's voice actually held a hint of yearning, not the condescending tone a city person might use about a country bumpkin's quaint ways.

Sweet Everything overflowed with customers. Most were people Liz didn't recognize, likely here for the dog show. Naomi bounced about filling orders, totally in her element. She declined joining them since the store was so busy, but Opal Ringenberg, another of the Material Girls, was in the shop buying cupcakes and Sadie managed to coax her to tag along.

They stopped by Sadie's house next to retrieve her camera, and by the time they got to the fairgrounds, the tracking trials had begun in one of the adjoining fields.

Opal tucked her silky scarf into the collar of her jacket and then pulled on thin gloves. "They're fortunate to have such mild weather this late in the season. I remember years when we already had snow on the ground by now."

Amy pointed out John Baxter and Peanut.

"They make an adorable pair," Mary Ann said.

"Yeah, isn't the little guy a cutie?" Liz said.

"Hmm," Amy crooned, pressing her palm to her chest. "Those warm brown eyes and that dimpled smile would melt the ice off a glacier."

"What?" Liz's attention jerked from Peanut to Amy, who was giving their dark-haired guest a thorough once-over. "I'm talking about the dog."

Amy spared him a glance. "Oh, yeah, he's cute too."

"I like the way your friend thinks," Sadie whispered close to Liz's ear. "You should take a page from her book," she added with a wink.

Mary Ann swatted Sadie's arm. "Leave her alone. She's going out with Jackson tonight."

"*Pfft*. Inviting Liz to accompany him to a play at the high school is hardly a date. If our handsome mayor hadn't been asked to give opening remarks, he probably wouldn't even go."

"Let's just watch the trials, okay?" Liz said.

Sadie snapped pictures as a border collie, with her handler in tow, raced across the field, nose to the ground, stopping only when she came upon one of the items that had been laid for her to find.

Based on the thunderous applause as the dog and her owner left the field, they were likely the pair to beat. John left his spot along the sidelines and shook the man's hand, engaging him in conversation for the entire length of time of the next competitor's race.

Then Peanut's turn arrived. Unfortunately, he seemed more interested in the tantalizing smells wafting from the outdoor hot dog cart near the building's back entrance than in any competition.

"I don't think that little dog knows how this event works," Sadie said.

"His owner either," Mary Ann interjected. "He's paying more attention to the people on the sidelines than his dog."

Liz tracked John's gaze to a group of men in business suits.

"Are those more judges?" Sadie pointed her camera lens at the crowd of spectators, and Liz heard it buzz as her friend zoomed in. "A business suit isn't exactly spectator attire."

"You'd be surprised," Opal chimed in. "The competitors in the conformation classes dress their best."

Liz returned her attention to the tracking trial. The judge gave Peanut an incomplete. The announcer summoned the next contestant, and John headed toward the building with Peanut. He didn't look terribly dejected at his dog's poor performance.

Loud applause broke out from the soccer field on the far side of the parking lot. Opal stood on her tiptoes and craned her neck to see over heads. "Let's check out what's going on over there."

"I'll catch up with you in a minute," Amy said. "I want to say hi to John and Peanut."

"I'll keep you company," Liz said as John and his beagle bypassed the hot dog cart and ducked under a rope circling a group of boxy tents.

A sign in big, red block letters on the side of one of the tents designated it *For Competitors Only*. John sauntered into the tent beside it that said *Staff Only*.

Amy headed straight for the opening in the rope.

Liz caught her arm and pointed out the signs, just as a burly guy, in a dark *Event Security* vest, returned from the concession area.

His gaze slid past them as he stepped over the rope.

"He doesn't scare me," Amy scoffed. "*Carpe diem*—seize the day—is my motto. The worst the guard can do is ask me to leave, right?"

"Sure," Liz countered. She jerked her chin toward John. "But it looks as if John's a tad preoccupied at the moment anyway."

Flashing his charming smile, he handed a pretty blonde his business card.

"Huh," Amy said, "what do you suppose—"

"Stop right there." The security guard set his large soda cup and food container on a table and stalked toward them.

"What did we do?" Liz asked, startled.

The guard strode right past them, zeroing in on a woman who'd apparently slipped in to the restricted area without authorization.

The woman innocently lifted her hands in surrender. Then as the security guard blasted her about reading signs, she twined a hank of her pastel-streaked hair around her finger and plastered on a "woe is me" pout.

Amy shot Liz a wry smirk. "Just about every one of my female clients tries that pout on the DA, hoping to talk him into a sweet deal. Never works."

The guard didn't fall for it either. He escorted her out of the cordoned-off area, depositing her near Liz and Amy.

Liz offered the woman an empathetic smile. "That guard sure takes his job seriously. That was almost us."

The woman snorted. "Yeah, what's the big deal?"

"Those boots are fabulous," Amy gushed, ogling the woman's footwear.

The woman grinned at the compliment. "Thank you."

"Prada, right?" As if Amy, who bought new footwear every other week, had to ask. "Can I ask where you got them?"

The woman's gaze swept past the guard to the tents, before returning to Amy. "Online auction?" she said, making it sound like a question.

Amy complimented her on her great find, and the woman, whose attention had already returned to the area that apparently contained whomever she was looking for, excused herself.

"She totally stole those boots," Amy muttered.

Considering Amy worked in criminal law, it didn't surprise Liz that Amy would be skeptical of the woman's story.

"I mean, her clothes are at least five years old. And it looks as if her kid sister streaked her hair, but she's wearing this season's super-expensive boots?"

Liz scrutinized the departing woman's feet. "They could be knockoffs and she was too embarrassed to admit it."

"I suppose." Amy returned her attention to where John had been conversing with the blonde, but he was gone.

The tall, bald handler of the border collie who'd burned up the tracking trials course had slid into John's place. But the woman didn't appear nearly as eager to chat with him.

A voice spoke inches from Liz's ear. "What are you doing?"

Liz jumped at the question before she registered Sadie's voice. She turned to see Sadie, and Opal standing next to her. "We were trying to catch up to my guest, John, but we lost sight of him. What are these tents for anyway?"

"This tent is a place for competitors to touch up their dog's appearance." Opal flipped through the pages of her program, then pointed to the far tent. "And that one is a lounge for the judges." She turned the page so Liz could view the map. The facing page held the names and photos of all the judges. "I'm sure they would've preferred a place further removed from the competitors," Opal went on. "You should've seen the Chihuahua owner back there lambasting one of the judges because of the score he gave her dog. The judge was in the right, of course."

"I guess that's why they take their security so seriously," Amy mused. "Ah well, we can catch up to John later. Let's watch another show. I was hoping to see the musical expression event."

Opal consulted her program. "That's starting right now in the arena inside."

"Great, let's go," Liz said and led the women through the less-crowded side entrance.

Amy seemed immediately captivated by the show, but Liz struggled to stay focused. Maybe it was because Sadie had just snuck up on her, but the back of her neck tingled with the sensation of being watched.

2

At the inn a few hours later, a couple of guests were already milling about outside the sitting room. Liz started preparing the coffee and tea service to go along with the afternoon goodies she'd promised them.

"I'll put the cookie platters and cups out for you," Amy said. "Then if you don't mind, I think I'll lie down for a while. All this fresh air seems to have worn me out."

Since the door to Liz's quarters was off the kitchen, Amy would have to pass through again to head for a nap. When she didn't, Liz figured John had arrived. Just then the sound of Amy talking with someone carried from the rotunda and Liz couldn't resist the impulse to meander out.

Only the man Amy was talking to wasn't John. A gray-haired gentleman in a dark overcoat hurried toward the front door.

"May I help you?" Liz called after him.

He either didn't hear or pretended not to and kept on going.

"Who was that?" Liz asked Amy.

"Someone looking for Ms. Hunt. She's the woman with the chow chow, right?"

"Yes, Gloria Hunt."

Amy nodded. "I thought so. I told him she wasn't back from the dog show yet. So he said he'd try to catch her there."

Liz frowned at the door. Maybe that explained why he was in such a hurry. "Did he go upstairs?"

"He looked as if he was about to head up when I stopped him. I didn't recognize him and figured you didn't let just anyone wander around on the upper floors."

"No, preferably not. Thanks."

After Amy retired to Liz's private quarters, Liz set the teapot and freshly brewed coffee on a tray, then headed to the sitting room. As she passed through the rotunda, John arrived with Peanut.

"Hey, sorry about the tracking trial," Liz said. "Was that Peanut's first time in competition?"

"That obvious, huh?"

Liz smiled encouragingly. "I'm sure he'll get the hang of it with more practice. Come join the guests for refreshments."

"Here, let me help you with that." John relieved her of the tray and followed her to the sitting room. Nodding to the assembled guests, he set it on the sideboard.

Tiffany and Tara cheered, set down the poodles, and immediately filled their mugs. The silver-haired, buxom Gloria Hunt arrived with her well-coiffed chow chow and complimented Liz on the selection of baked goodies. Edward Lock, owner of an adorable shih tzu, greeted John and patted Peanut affectionately.

But Rhonda Piper, an attractive woman of about thirty-five, shot John a look so caustic, Liz expected him to shrivel on the spot.

Oh man. Liz had feared there might be a bit of rivalry amongst her guests, but Rhonda wasn't even a competitor at the dog show.

John graced the woman with a heart-stopping smile. "Miss Piper, you're looking well."

Rhonda dropped her gaze to her tea, downed it in one long gulp, then abruptly stood and excused herself.

An awkward silence descended on the room, casting a shadow over what was usually an opportunity for the guests to get to know each other. Clearly Rhonda and John already knew each other—too well.

Liz passed a plate of lemon bars to Gloria. "There was a gentleman looking for you a few minutes ago. Did you run into him outside?"

Gloria looked as if she couldn't imagine who he'd be. "Did he say what he wanted?"

"No, I didn't actually talk to him. My friend did. She suggested he look for you at the dog show. I'm sure he'll catch up to you sooner or later."

"Hmm."

Once again the guests fell silent.

"Have all of you met at other dog shows?" Liz asked.

Tiffany and Tara shook their heads.

"Edward and I have participated in a few of the same shows," Gloria replied.

"Have you competed with other dogs before Peanut?" Liz asked John. Although Peanut had clearly been a greenhorn, John had seemed well acquainted with the judges' corner of the field.

"No. This was a first for both of us. Trust me, Peanut does much better at home." He ruffled Peanut's floppy ears. "He's not used to the extra distractions here." John's gaze slid to the doorway Rhonda had stormed through moments earlier. "If you'll excuse me, I think I'll go outside and toss the ball with Peanut for a while."

At the word *ball*, Peanut perked up, and Edward's little shih tzu whined longingly.

"Sorry, bub," Edward consoled. "It's too dirty out there. Maybe we can do a few ball rolls down the hall outside our room?" He looked to Liz for permission.

The upstairs rooms ringed the hallway, which in turn circled the open rotunda at the inn's center, not exactly the safest place to roll a ball. But Edward was in the Amish Room, tucked into the corner.

"In the area above the foyer, rather than along the hall, would be better, as long as it doesn't bother the other guests."

The shih tzu did a little dance as if he'd understood her. Edward grinned. "I guess my tea break is over too. Thank you. The lemon bars were delicious."

He stood and, crooking his arm, looked down at his dog. "Coming?"

The dog sprang from the couch into his master's arms and they headed upstairs.

Gloria snorted an almost imperceptible, but unmistakably disapproving sound. Her chow chow sat next to her chair looking as stately and prim as his owner, not being the type of dog who would ever do anything so playful, even if he were fifty pounds lighter.

Gloria pushed her cup and saucer to the center of the table and patted her lips with her napkin. "Has that young woman who stormed out earlier been here before?"

"No," Liz said.

"Well, you might want to keep your eye on her," Gloria warned in a confidential tone. "These competitions, especially large regional events like this one, tend to attract a few radicals."

"Oh?" Visions of placard-carrying protestors circling the inn rose in Liz's mind.

Tiffany and Tara nodded vigorously, their poodles seeming to imitate them.

"But you all clearly adore your animals." Liz petted the poodle that nuzzled her hand. "What do they hope to gain?"

"Media coverage, mostly," Gloria said.

Terrific. Liz could see the headline now—*Stunt Planned While Sipping Tea at the Olde Mansion Inn and Eavesdropping on Competitors' Conversations.*

Tiffany and Tara withdrew as Gloria regaled Liz with a few such stunts from previous competitions, and Liz found herself listening for the creaks of floorboards from anyone who might be listening in. But the only sounds she heard were the playful romps of Edward's shih tzu on the floor overhead and Peanut's happy yelps outside.

Gloria's chow chow eventually persuaded the talkative woman

that a visit to the great outdoors would be a good idea for them too.

When she left, Liz stood at the kitchen sink and watched John through the window as he attempted to entice Beans, who'd followed John and Peanut outside then promptly plopped himself on the steps, to join in their game of catch.

She probably should make more of an effort to get Beans to exercise. He was the laziest dog she knew.

Rhonda stalked across the yard toward John and her raised voice pierced the window—not well enough for Liz to make out what she'd said, but her rigid stance and fisted hands made it clear that whatever it was wasn't friendly.

John's charming smile remained intact as he held up open hands and said something that seemed conciliatory.

Liz couldn't make out Rhonda's response, even though it'd been sharp enough to jerk Beans to his feet. He sidled his rump next to John's leg and aimed a wary glance at the hysterical woman. Liz dried the dishwater from her hands and headed for the door to nip in the bud whatever was going on.

She traversed the four-season room that opened to the yard and pushed open the screen door.

Rhonda's gaze snapped to Liz. Then Rhonda poked a finger into John's chest and hissed, "I'd better not see you anywhere near me again."

Beans let out a loud woof, like a referee calling a foul.

Rhonda scowled at him then strode off in the opposite direction.

John stooped down and gave Beans an affectionate rub. "It's okay, boy." If he'd noticed Liz watching from the back stoop, he didn't let on. He probably didn't want to talk about what the deal was between him and Rhonda. And if it didn't result in any more outbursts, Liz supposed it was none of her business, so she slipped back inside to finish the dishes.

A few minutes later, John came in with Peanut in his arms. "Hey, could you do me a favor?"

"What's that?"

"Could I leave Peanut here with you for half an hour or so?"

Liz's thoughts flashed to Rhonda. "Is everything okay?" What if he planned to hunt down alternative accommodation to avoid her?

"Everything's fine. But I have a few errands to run, and Peanut hates being trucked around. He won't give you any trouble. Will probably sleep. He's pretty worn out after all the people today."

Peanut gave her a pleading look with eyes no one with a heart could resist.

"Sure. He can nap while I work on my computer." Liz hung up the dishcloth. "This way." She showed him to the library and pointed to a rug. "You can put him there."

"Perfect." He commanded Peanut to sit on the rug and in a stern voice said, "Now you be good. Stay right here."

"I'm sure he'll be fine," Liz reassured John when he seemed to waver over his decision to leave the dog.

"Thanks. I appreciate this." He dug his keys from his pocket and hurried out.

Liz turned on her computer, but before she had a chance to get to work, the sound of someone stomping through the front door drew her out to the foyer.

Rhonda closed the door with deliberate slowness. It was clear she would have preferred to slam it. "That man is lower than pond scum."

Mary Ann wandered in from Sew Welcome, no doubt also curious about the commotion. "Oh trust me, dear," she said, "we all feel that way about our husbands from time to time. But things will get better. You'll see. You just—"

"He's not my husband," Rhonda snapped. "A woman would have to be an idiot to marry him."

Sadie meandered in, her gaze bouncing from Rhonda, now stomping up the stairs, to Mary Ann then Liz. "What did the guy do?" Sadie asked. "Leave her for another woman?"

"I don't know," Liz whispered.

"Is she a dog show contestant?" Mary Ann asked. "Maybe his dog spooked hers out of contention."

John's beagle emerged from the library, looking a tad indignant. Or as indignant as a beagle could look with those adorable floppy ears.

"She didn't mean it, Peanut," Liz soothed. "She didn't know."

"Is that the man's dog?" Sadie interjected. "He looks like the type who could get into a lot of mischief. It would explain your guest's reaction. These dog show people take the competition very seriously."

"I don't think Rhonda is a competitor." Liz tried to shoo Peanut back into the library. "She doesn't have a dog with her."

"You're probably right," Mary Ann said. "I've heard owners don't like to let their dogs out of their sight. Jealous competitors have been known to resort to sabotage to ensure they win."

Sadie glanced into the library. "Then where is this little guy's owner?"

Liz scooped Peanut into her arms. "He asked me to watch him while he runs errands."

Rhonda, a large designer purse flung over her shoulder, hurried back down the stairs and went out through the front door.

"It's a good thing that woman didn't spot the dog," Mary Ann said. "I wouldn't want her to start scolding the little fellow for his master's faults."

"Or kidnap him," Sadie interjected.

"I hadn't thought about that." Mary Ann glanced about nervously. "You'd better keep a close eye on him."

"This is Pleasant Creek, not New York City. I'm sure the dog will be safe." Liz returned to her computer to get started on her accounting duties. But as "half an hour" slipped into a full hour, then two, then three, with no sign of John, she wondered if, although the dog was safe, she might not be able to say the same for his owner.

3

At seven o'clock, the bell on Liz's reception desk dinged.

"That'll be Jackson," Liz said to Amy and hurried out of her private quarters, with her cell phone pressed to her ear and Peanut on her heels. John didn't answer. Again. "One second," she whispered to Pleasant Creek's popular mayor, Jackson Cross, as John's voice mail recording kicked on for the dozenth time.

At the sound of his master's voice on the phone, Peanut's ears perked up.

The recording ended, and Liz said into the phone, "This is Liz again. Is everything okay? I have a da—" She glanced at Jackson, uncertain whether he considered this a date, since, as Sadie had said, his attendance was more of a mayoral obligation than a night on the town. "I have somewhere else I need to be," she amended. "Very soon. Please call me back as soon as you get this."

"Problem?" Jackson kneeled and petted Peanut. "Aren't you cute?"

The dog wagged his tail, and his entire back end with it, as he lapped up Jackson's attention. Beans, who'd been lounging near the reception desk, nosed in, demanding equal treatment.

Liz grinned at them. *Man's best friend indeed.* Though Beans had certainly been there when she'd needed him in the past.

Then she glanced at the clock. Curtain time was a mere twenty-five minutes away. "I promised one of my guests I'd watch his dog for him. He was supposed to be back within an hour, but it's been almost four and I can't reach him on his cell phone. I don't know what to do."

Amy traipsed through the rotunda carrying a tray of tea and cookies for the evening's Material Girls quilting session, which Liz was missing in favor of attending the high school's theatrical performance of *Brigadoon*. "I can watch Peanut for you."

Liz quickly made introductions.

Jackson stood and swiped ineffectively at the white fur that now covered his dark trousers. He grimaced. "You might want to make sure he stays away from the fabric."

"Are you sure you don't mind?" Liz asked Amy, already feeling bad about leaving her friend on her own when it was only her second night in town.

"Of course I don't." Amy's eyes twinkled, clearly telling Liz, *You know I'd do whatever it takes to ensure you don't miss your date.* "We'll be fine. C'mon, Peanut."

Peanut sniffed at the tray of goodies and trotted after Amy without so much as a glance over his shoulder. Not about to be left out of potential treats, Beans trailed them.

Liz chuckled. "And here I thought Peanut would be upset if I abandoned him after his owner stayed away so long." Liz pulled her coat from the closet. "Do you think he's okay? You haven't heard about any car accidents or anything in the area, have you?"

Jackson took her coat and held it up for her to slip into. "I haven't heard a siren all evening. He probably got reminiscing with an old friend and lost track of time."

Liz inhaled a deep breath, trying to calm her doubts. "You're right." She hoped.

As Jackson and Liz stepped outside, Rhonda climbed the porch stairs, looking much happier than she had when she left.

Jackson's "Good evening" earned him a smile.

"Yes, it is, isn't it?" Rhonda crossed the porch with a spring in her step.

"I'll be back in a couple of hours," Liz said. "If you need anything in the interim, the ladies in Sew Welcome can assist you."

Rhonda waved Liz off. "I'll be fine."

Jackson held open the passenger door of his car and waited for Liz to cross the driveway.

"I'm so sorry to keep you waiting," she said.

"Remember, I'm a business owner too," he said. He shipped handcrafted wood furniture worldwide from Cross Furniture Company. Many of her guests included a visit to his shop in their plans. "I understand these things happen." He guided her into his truck with a fleeting touch to the small of her back, warming her from top to toe even through her fleece jacket.

The high school auditorium was packed by the time they arrived. The principal visibly relaxed the instant he spotted Jackson walking down the center aisle. He met him at the base of the stage. "We're ready to begin. If you'll join me on stage now, you can give your opening remarks."

"I just need to find Liz a seat first."

The principal snapped his fingers at one of the student ushers. "Could you find a seat for Miss Eckardt and the mayor?"

The girl scanned the auditorium and although there was an odd empty seat here and there, there didn't appear to be two together.

"If you can find a couple of chairs to add to the back row, that will be fine," Liz said.

"That's okay," the girl said. "I just found two empty seats in row seven."

Liz spied the pair of seats, separated by three rambunctious students, and Sadie's *attending a high school play is hardly a date* remark drifted through her mind. She bit back a smirk. Amy would be disappointed to hear Liz didn't even get to sit beside Jackson.

"Perfect," the principal said and hustled Jackson onto the stage.

The girl led Liz down the aisle, then leaned over the nearest students to the three beyond the first empty seat. "Could you three move over a seat, so we can have two seats together?"

The students bounced up and cheerfully shifted over a seat, but that didn't stop Liz's cheeks from flaming as she wedged her way past the knees of the audience members between her and her seat. Nothing like drawing attention to her tardiness by inconveniencing everyone else.

The audience quieted, except for a flurry of whispers Liz sincerely hoped weren't about her. Setting her coat on the chair before taking her seat, she thanked the girl who'd relinquished it for her.

"No problem."

Liz saw a flash near the girl's nose. She had a nose ring. Liz's mom hadn't even let her get her ears pierced at that age, which seemed tame by comparison. Liz smothered a laugh at the idea of her teenage self asking her mother, who had been raised Amish, even though Liz didn't know it at the time, if she could pierce her nose.

The auditorium lights dimmed and Jackson settled into the seat beside her. She hadn't even registered his opening address.

He smiled at her. "Everything okay?"

"Absolutely."

Within minutes of the band striking up its first song, Liz was swept up in the story and all other thoughts fled. The students did an amazing job. The sets were exquisite and the songs fun, with a few of the actors taking comical license here and there. Liz enjoyed it so much she led the standing ovation as the curtain fell. "Oh, Jackson, thank you so much for inviting me. I had no idea the students were so talented."

"My pleasure." He snuck her out a side door to avoid the crowds and held open the car door for her. "Mind if we take the scenic route home? It's a beautiful night."

"Sounds good to me."

He soon pulled out of the parking lot, and she fixed her gaze on the passing scenery, as Sadie's *"attending a high school play is hardly a date"* replayed in her thoughts once more.

Sadie had clearly never seen *Brigadoon*. The entire musical was about love and seizing the moment when you find it. Of course, when you find your true love in a village that's only visible once every hundred years, the impetus to act on your feelings immediately must be a whole lot stronger.

Not that Liz had the urge to hurry her relationship with Jackson. They had agreed to take it slow.

Still, as she'd watched the show, she couldn't help but draw parallels to her own situation—like leaving a wannabe fiancé behind in the city and finding an idyllic life here in Pleasant Creek.

Jackson drove along the winding river road. "I love how the moonlight sparkles on the water, don't you?"

His comment had startled her from her thoughts. "Uh, yes, it's a beautiful night," she replied lamely.

She seriously needed to learn how to flirt. No wonder guys didn't ask her on real dates anymore.

Then again, was that what she wanted?

The last guy who'd wanted to marry her had turned out to be a self-absorbed jerk. She didn't know how she hadn't seen it sooner. Not that dating had to lead to marriage.

Liz's mind drifted back to the play, to the look on the main character's face when he was told he had to leave Brigadoon unless he loved someone enough to give up everything to stay with that person. "Which is how it should be," the man had said.

"Whoa, what's going on up there?" Jackson's voice cut into Liz's thoughts again, and her gaze snapped to the windshield.

Red and blue lights strobed across the glass in an eerie glow. Barricades cut off the road. Beyond them, police cars, an ambulance, and a fire truck lined the road. A ten-foot-high floodlight illuminated the adjacent field.

"I don't see any wrecked cars or a tow truck," Liz said.

Jackson stopped at the barricade and shifted his car into park. "Wait here." He jumped out and headed straight for the group of emergency personnel at the center of the light-drenched scene.

A police officer at first blocked his path, but then he must've recognized him as the mayor and waved him through. When the police chief, Stan Houghton, turned toward Jackson, Liz glimpsed a body bag.

Tell me that's not John.

Liz bolted from the truck and approached the scene. The chief waved her toward the gurney now holding the body bag. "Jackson tells me you have a missing guest who might be our victim."

Liz swallowed hard. "Yes," she croaked.

"He left his dog in Liz's care this afternoon and said he'd only be away an hour," Jackson filled in. "But he hadn't returned by the time we left the inn, several hours later."

The chief nodded then studied Liz for a long, solemn moment. "The victim's wallet is missing, so we haven't been able to identify him yet. Do you think you could take a look?"

Liz's stomach rolled. But it had to be done.

Jackson squeezed her shoulder. "It's okay if you're not up to it."

"No. I'm fine. I will."

The chief nodded to the EMT manning the head of the gurney, and the woman unzipped the top of the body bag.

Liz drew in an abrupt breath. "It's not him. But—"

"Do you recognize him?"

She pressed her palm to her pounding chest. "He looks familiar." Unable to tear her gaze away from the lifeless face, she mentally clambered through her memory bank, desperate to remember why.

She turned on her heel and ran back to the truck for her purse. She dug through it, found the dog show program, and quickly thumbed to the page showcasing the judges' photos. "Yes." She raced back to the chief. "It's William Purcell. He's one of the dog show judges. Was one," she corrected.

The chief exchanged a rueful glance with the mayor. "Not exactly how you hoped to put Pleasant Creek on the map."

Jackson looked haggard. "Do your best to keep the details out of the press." He clasped Liz by the arm and steered her away from the crime scene.

Numbered cards were propped about on the ground, marking the location of potential evidence, she supposed. Scarcely any blood stained the ground. There'd been no bruises on the man's face. "Did Stan tell you how he died?" Liz asked.

Jackson opened his passenger door for her. "Stabbed in the back. They haven't located the weapon yet."

She nodded and stepped toward Jackson's car, suddenly exhausted.

He stopped her with a brush of his thumb across her damp cheek. "Hey, your guest will turn up. He's probably already back at the inn."

"Yeah." She couldn't muster enough enthusiasm to make him think she believed it. But at least her guest wasn't dead—that they knew of. She tamped down the morbid thought. "Why would anyone want to kill a dog show judge? Are people really that desperate to win these things?"

"I don't know."

Liz nodded. There was no point in speculating. They hadn't even known him. But that didn't stop a thick pall from hanging over her on the drive home.

"John could've had car trouble," Jackson suggested. "If his phone died, it would explain why you couldn't reach him and why he couldn't call for help."

"I guess." It could happen. And she didn't know if the Amish on these roads shared a phone for business and emergencies as some did. But Liz struggled to scrounge up enough hope to believe it.

"It's pretty easy to get lost on the back roads. Even I've gotten turned around a time or two, and I've lived here all my life. I remember one of my first times driving on my own. I ended up way out at the Fergusons' old hunting cabin, before I realized I was on the opposite side of the county from where I'd thought."

"Hmm." Surely by now someone would've picked John up and given him a lift to the inn, considering how kind and generous Pleasant Creek residents were.

Jackson turned his vehicle into her driveway.

"A light's on in John's room." Liz's heart lightened. "You must've been right."

But as Jackson pulled up near the door and stopped, Peanut burst from the shadows, tugging Amy, not John, at the other end of his lead.

Liz jumped out of the car. "Where's John?"

"Not back yet."

"But—" Liz backstepped and peered up at his now-dark second-story window. It must've been the reflection of Jackson's headlights she'd seen a moment ago.

"How was the play?" Amy asked.

"As fabulous as you said it would be."

Amy grinned. "It's one of my favorites."

Liz glanced at the window once more. "Has John called?"

"No, why?" Amy asked.

Liz stepped close to her friend and lowered her voice. "There's been a murder."

"What?" Amy yelped.

"Shhh! It wasn't John. But it was someone connected to the dog show."

Amy frowned. "It's been quiet here all evening. The last of your Material Girls left a few minutes ago."

Liz released a pent-up breath and relieved Amy of Peanut's leash. "I appreciate you watching him."

"No trouble. He's a cutie. Almost makes me want to have a pup of my own."

Beans rounded the corner of the house and let out a disgruntled snort.

Amy chuckled. "I'm afraid he's had his nose out of joint all evening. The ladies were showing Peanut far too much attention for Beans's liking. Although Sadie did make a fuss over him."

"She always does." Liz shook her head at her dog. "If you cared about more than eating and sleeping, the rest of the girls might fuss over you too, you know."

Beans plopped on his rump and tilted his head, as if giving the notion serious consideration.

Liz ruffled his fur. "You're a sweetheart too."

"Why don't you try your guest's cell phone again?" Jackson suggested.

Liz found her last call to John and hit redial, then paced the lawn, listening to it ring.

The ringing abruptly stopped and the line connected, but John didn't say anything.

Was that a whistle? Liz pressed the phone to her ear, wondering if it was a bad connection. She could hear muffled sounds of country music, people, and what sounded like the low rumble of a train. "Hello, John? It's Liz. Are you okay?"

"Sorry, lady." The brash voice sounded as if it belonged to a male teenager. "You've got the wrong number."

No. She didn't. That was the same number she'd dialed umpteen times today and been sent to John's voicemail.

Liz's heart pounded. "Who is this?" *And what are you doing with John's phone?*

He disconnected.

"No, wait!"

Jackson and Amy lurched toward her as one. "What's wrong?"

"Something's happened to John."

4

Liz went through the motions of her breakfast-making routine in a bleary-eyed haze. She'd had a restless night worrying about John. She'd called Chief Houghton to let him know about someone else answering John's phone, but he'd been too busy investigating last night's murder to get excited about a man who'd been missing less than twelve hours. Never mind that John had said he'd return in less than one. She gave him the home address John had used when he registered. The chief promised to look into it.

Her guests arrived in the dining room en masse shortly after eight and heaped their plates with fresh fruit, homemade muffins, bacon, eggs, and home fries at the buffet.

"Did you hear the news about the murdered judge?" Edward, the shih tzu owner, asked Liz. "It was all over the radio this morning."

"Did you know him?" Liz asked.

"Not personally. But he's judged quite a few events and trials we've been in at various shows. He prefers conformation, which is where the dog is physically examined for the breed's desired traits."

"Ever hear anyone threaten him?"

"Not to his face. But plenty of dog owners get bent out of shape when their dogs get a low score." Edward loaded bacon and eggs on his plate. "I could see one of them lashing out at the offending judge at an opportune moment."

Gloria nodded. "Mr. Purcell is—I mean, was one of the harsher judges. He'd ticked off quite a few owners, not to mention

33

breeders, with his favoritism for toy dogs. Frankly, I'm surprised these shows continued inviting him back."

Edward shrugged. "I thought he was a pretty good judge."

"This from the owner of a toy dog," Rhonda said, setting a plate of scrambled eggs on the table beside Edward.

"None of the other breeds had a hope of winning Best in Show with Purcell on the roster, that's for sure," Gloria added. "I wouldn't put it past one of the breeders to have taken matters into his own hands to ensure a fair competition."

Amy bypassed the sideboard of food and headed straight for the coffeepot. "In my experience, murders are usually over an unpaid gambling debt, criminal activity, or an argument with one's partner."

"In your *experience*?" Rhonda needled. "You don't even know the guy and you're saying his death is his own fault?"

Amy gaped at her, no doubt thinking—as Liz was—that the others hadn't exactly been touting the man's finer qualities either.

"Amy is a criminal lawyer," Liz explained. She poured herself a cup of coffee too, hoping the caffeine would give her a much-needed energy boost.

"How interesting," Tiffany gushed to Amy. "Have you defended murderers?"

Amy winced. "I've assisted in the defense of suspects accused of murder."

Edward toasted her with his coffee mug. "Spoken like a true lawyer."

"You think the police got it wrong?" Tara interjected. "I mean, I know it happens, but is it common for the police to arrest the wrong guy?"

"I wouldn't say 'common,' no."

Liz mouthed "sorry" to Amy for inadvertently putting her in the hot seat. At least no one was asking about John. If they figured out he'd disappeared within hours of Purcell's death, they'd have a speculation heyday. She hated that she was already thinking John might've been involved somehow.

Liz carried the empty coffeepot back to the kitchen and started another pot. While she waited, she poured food for Beans and Peanut into their respective bowls. Peanut looked at her with sad, brown eyes and whined. "He'll be back. Don't you worry," she said, as much for her own benefit as the dog's.

A tap sounded at the back door.

"Chief, thank you so much for coming." There were definitely perks to having friends in high places. She'd expected the chief to send an officer to look into John's disappearance, not come himself. "I know it hasn't been twenty-four hours since my guest went missing, but with this other man having been found murdered, I'm really worried."

"That's what I'm here about."

"Do you have any leads? Were you able to get a location on John's cell number? Find anyone at the address I gave you? I'm afraid John paid cash, so—"

"Liz, stop. Sit down."

Her heart stumbled at his uncharacteristic abruptness.

He must've read her confusion, because he pulled out a kitchen chair and added in a placating tone, "Please."

This can't be good. "Did you already find him?" Fearing the worst, she couldn't hide the quaver in her voice.

The chief set a box on the table in front of Liz and opened it. "Do you recognize this knife?"

Liz's breath caught at the sight of blood on the old-fashioned Amish corn knife that looked a lot like her own. Her gaze tripped over a notch in the handle, which matched a mar in hers. She leaned in closer to study it, being careful to avoid touching it and adding her fingerprints. But she had a sinking feeling the chief had already found them all over it. She was pretty sure it was her knife.

"Where did you find this? Is that Purcell's blood?" Her mind scrambled to remember where she'd last laid it down.

"You recognize the knife?"

"Clearly you've already figured out it belongs to me or you wouldn't be here showing it to me. I used it yesterday to cut evergreen branches to bring inside." Searching her memory, she added, "I was out front with it when John Baxter arrived." Liz squinted, trying to recall what she'd done with it after that. She didn't remember going back to the toolshed. She'd led John inside. She sprang up and led the way to the reception desk.

She pointed to a small table. "I laid it here just before checking John in. That was early yesterday afternoon and the last time I saw it."

Sarah came down the stairs at that moment, carrying a bundle of sheets.

"Sarah, did you move the corn knife I left here yesterday?" Liz asked as the chief stood by watching the exchange in silence.

"No, I haven't seen it. Maybe your friend returned it to the toolshed."

"I doubt she would have," Liz said to Stan. "Whoever picked it up must've taken it from here." She hugged her arms to ward off a sudden chill, since this meant chances were way too high that a guest had "borrowed" the knife. "I guess John is your prime suspect."

"He saw you lay the knife there?"

"Yes."

Stan blew out a weary-sounding sigh. "My men found the knife in the bushes near where Purcell's body was discovered. The blood is Purcell's."

Liz's heart slammed in her chest. Someone had used her knife to kill a man.

She recounted a timeline of her afternoon following John's arrival. "If only I'd remembered to put the knife away before we left for the dog show," she lamented.

"Then the murderer would've found a different weapon," Stan

said grimly. "The weapon went missing from the inn, and the body was found miles away. This was premeditated."

"Any other prints on the knife?"

He shook his head. "I know you didn't kill Purcell—"

"Glad to hear it." She didn't think he would see her as a suspect, but the "but" in his tone made her a tad uneasy.

"But for the sake of a thorough investigation"—he steered her back to the kitchen and pulled out his notebook and pen—"we need to verify your alibi. Where were you yesterday between the hours of four and six p.m.?"

"Here, working in the library."

"Can anyone verify that?"

"Sure, my friend Amy. Sarah. Sadie and Mary Ann. Probably even some of my guests."

"Good. That's good. I'll need a list of your guests and anyone else who could've lifted the knife from your reception area."

Liz muffled a resigned sigh. She'd known he'd ask, but it didn't make it any easier to take. "Do you really think one of my guests killed Purcell? Didn't he have other enemies?"

"Someone helped themselves to the knife after you set it down yesterday afternoon. And that someone must've been wearing gloves, because if they'd wiped down the knife to clear away their own prints yours would've been wiped clean too."

"Lots of guests wear gloves." Winter wouldn't officially arrive for a couple more weeks, and they'd been enjoying unseasonably warm weather this year, but the air was still nippy.

"Did Mr. Baxter wear gloves?"

"Yes," Amy interjected, entering the kitchen with a tray of empty plates. "He was wearing a gorgeous pair of brown kid-leather gloves." She smiled at Liz. "He removed his right glove before shaking my hand. He had a nice firm grip too. You can tell a lot about a man by the way he shakes your hand."

"And you are?" the chief asked.

"This is my friend, Amy Cooper, from Boston. She's a criminal lawyer," Liz said, as if that should wipe away any suspicions that she had something to do with Purcell's murder.

"I see. And had you met Mr. Baxter before yesterday?" the chief asked Amy.

"No."

"What about William Purcell?"

"The judge who was killed? No."

"Where were you between four and six p.m. yesterday afternoon?" the chief continued.

Liz shrank into her chair, knowing the question would be repeated to every single one of her guests, and the employees and clients of Sew Welcome. The fact that previous guests had endured the same treatment in other investigations didn't make the prospect any easier to accept.

"Napping on Liz's couch," Amy said.

Stan looked to Liz for confirmation.

Liz nodded. "I won't have a spare room for her until the weekend guests clear out." It wasn't that Liz had watched the door to her private quarters the entire afternoon and could say without a shadow of a doubt that Amy hadn't snuck out and sped off to murder some judge she didn't know, and then snuck back in. Liz shook away the ridiculous thought.

"I'd like to search Mr. Baxter's room," the chief said.

"Of course." Liz dug her master key out of her pocket, happy to refocus on finding her missing guest.

"I'll finish cleaning up for you," Amy offered.

Sarah appeared, carrying a stack of clean towels.

"Hold up there." Stan glanced from Liz to Sarah, who paused

at the doorway. "Has anyone been in Mr. Baxter's room since he left yesterday afternoon?"

Sarah shook her head. "I'm heading upstairs to freshen the rooms now."

"Skip Mr. Baxter's. I need to see it first." Stan strode to the wide staircase leading to the rooms on the upper level. "Which room?"

Liz hurried past him to lead the way. "He's in the Somewhere in Time Room. This way."

The chief trailed Liz up the stairs. "Did Mr. Baxter happen to mention who he was going to see yesterday?"

"No, but it had to be someone nearby. Like I told you last night, he expected to be gone only half an hour. You couldn't locate his phone?" She'd already asked this but he hadn't answered.

"The number you gave me has gone dark."

"That kid who answered it last night probably got scared he'd be caught for mugging him or something and turned it off." It was pretty tough to believe any kids around Pleasant Creek would mug a guy for a phone. More likely the kid found it dropped somewhere.

"We followed up with the phone company, but all they could tell us was the tower on the edge of town picked up the call. So he could've been in town or halfway to the next one."

"I'd give you John's credit card number to trace, but he paid cash in advance for his room."

"Cash, huh?"

"I know what you're thinking, but lots of guests pay cash. It doesn't mean he's a criminal." *Even though one or two cash-paying guests have been in the past.*

"Or that he isn't." Clearly the chief was remembering, as she was.

"True." She wasn't sure why she'd felt compelled to defend him, except that she hated to think any of her guests could be criminals. Besides which there was nothing wrong with paying cash. Never mind that it was what bank robbers and drug dealers and hired assassins would do. She buried her hands in the pockets of her hoodie and hovered in the doorway.

Stan tugged on a pair of latex gloves and surveyed the room.

Liz should've felt reassured that he was treating John's disappearance so seriously, but his grim demeanor left her feeling as if he already knew something more sinister about the man's disappearance.

Stan crossed the room and tipped open John's suitcase, which was empty. All of John's shirts and slacks hung in a neat row in the open closet. Stan mutely looked through them. It wasn't like him to be so tight-lipped. For as many cases as she'd helped solve around Pleasant Creek, one would think he'd welcome her interest.

"Was it *my* call to his phone that you got the tower location on?" Liz asked. "The one the teenager picked up? Because if you find the kid who took John's phone—"

"We're looking into it." He groaned and shot her a sheepish look. "Sorry, my head feels as if I've got a whole construction crew hammering inside it."

"Can I get you something for it?"

The chief slipped a small fingerprint kit from his pocket. "I'm okay, thanks. I took something before I came."

"I guess I'll leave you to your work then."

Walking away, Liz remembered the light she thought she'd seen through John's window when she arrived home last night. She bit her lip. The timing was long after the murder and John's disappearance. Should she bother the chief again when it had probably been the headlights bouncing off the window?

Except . . . she'd been sure it was a light. She returned to the doorway and filled him in on what she thought she'd seen. "But it couldn't have been the same person who answered John's phone," she added. "Because I called only minutes later and I could hear a train rumbling in the background and country music and other voices." Liz closed her eyes to help herself remember better. "There was a whistle blast too, just as the phone connected—like a train lets out when it passes an intersection."

He noted the information in his notebook. "You've got a good memory for details."

Rhonda came upstairs and, passing Liz, glanced into John's room, then hurried on to her own.

Interesting. Given the woman's hatred of John, wouldn't she have gloated over the chief's interest in his room? Unless . . .

Rhonda *knew* something about John's disappearance.

She had gone out soon after John yesterday afternoon. Liz cringed at the implication. She glanced at the chief. She couldn't point fingers at her guests without any evidence. After all, guests rarely stayed in during the day.

She recalled how happy Rhonda had been when she'd returned later. Were her troubles with John behind her? What if she'd made sure of it?

Liz crossed her arms to quiet her pounding heart. "When will you need to question the guests?"

"A couple of officers are on their way now."

"But you think John killed Purcell?"

Stan stopped what he was doing, and let out a long, impatient breath. "In my experience, when a grown man disappears, he's got something to hide. By your own admission, his whereabouts at the time of the murder are unaccounted for."

Liz's heart sank. "I just can't believe he'd leave Peanut behind. He adored the little fellow. And these dogs are valuable, right? The fact that John didn't come back for his dog before disappearing should be evidence enough he didn't leave by choice." Liz slid a glance down the hall to Rhonda's room.

"Or he figured the dog would make him too easy to find." Stan returned his attention to lifting prints. "Besides, Purcell's last call was to Mr. Baxter's number."

Oh. Well, that doesn't look good. Then again . . . "Maybe they knew each other. The call could mean we should be equally worried about John's fate. Some lunatic could be out there on a killing spree. You should—"

"I'm following the evidence," the chief interjected quietly but firmly—not at all how he usually treated her theories, but maybe it was just the headache. He scrutinized the prints he'd lifted. "The investigation is in its early stages yet."

At his conciliatory addendum, she dared to press for more details on the evidence he was following. "Did Purcell's phone have a recording? Something incriminating?"

"Liz, stay out of this, okay? And if Mr. Baxter returns, call me right away. Don't try to engage him."

Liz turned to leave. "Whatever you say." Well, except for the staying out of it part. But the man was not himself today, so why argue?

Stan stepped out of John's room and locked the door. "Tell Sarah not to clean it today. I may be back."

Still flabbergasted her missing guest had risen to fugitive status, Liz trailed Stan down the stairs.

Peanut scampered over to her and planted his paws on her legs. She directed him to sit with the hand signal she'd seen John use. He immediately complied.

"I can take the dog off your hands if you like," Stan said.

"And what? Drop him at the pound?" Liz couldn't allow that. Peanut whined.

"Absolutely not," Liz declared and scratched behind the dog's ears. "Don't worry, Peanut," she said consolingly. "Your master will come back for you. And I will take good care of you until he does."

Stan gave Liz a stern look. "Don't do anything foolish."

Liz opened her mouth to say more, then closed it again.

"And don't mention the knife to anyone. I want to suppress information about the weapon because we might be able to trip up the perpetrator that way."

Her heart thudded. She could picture the headline: *Innkeeper's Knife Used to Murder Dog Show Judge.* That was *not* the kind of publicity she wanted. She had to figure out the truth before someone leaked the info to reporters.

5

Stan handed his officers the guest list Liz had provided, then sent them off to start with Tiffany and Tara. Crossing the rotunda toward the foyer and the front door, he said to Liz, "Remember what I said. If Mr. Baxter returns, call me."

Mary Ann bustled in. "Did you hear? They found a bo—" Her gaze collided with the chief's and her face went white. "Oh dear, was it Liz's missing guest?"

"No," Stan said sharply. "And don't encourage her." With that, he jammed his cap back on his head and strode out. It seemed like the whole building shook when the door slammed behind him.

"Goodness! What did you do to get him so worked up?"

"I have no idea." She'd stuck her nose into more than a few of his cases and it'd never bothered him this way before. Or at least, not to the extent it seemed to have bothered him today. "He said he had a headache." But the excuse didn't stop her from feeling more than a little hurt by his dismissal. "I asked too many questions, I guess."

"He should be used to that by now."

Liz managed to return her quip with a smile.

Mary Ann tugged Liz into her arms and hugged her. "You look as if you've lost your best friend. Don't worry. Your guest will come back, and the chief will be fine the next time you see him."

"Thanks."

"Breakfast is all cleaned up," Amy said, joining them in the front hall.

"I'd better get to the shop," Mary Ann said and retreated to Sew Welcome.

"So what's going on?" Amy asked.

Since Amy had already overheard the chief ask about the knife's whereabouts and been questioned herself, Liz told her the whole story.

"John's not a murderer," Amy declared, her conviction presumably based on nothing more than his dimpled smile and honest eyes. "Trust me, I know how to read criminals. Your chief should be investigating those big-dog breeders that complained about Purcell's toy-dog favoritism."

"I'm sure he's covering all the angles."

"Well, he can get off the John angle."

Liz smirked. "Are you sure you just don't want to believe you flirted with a criminal?"

Amy chuckled. "That too. But hey, life's too short to do a background check on every guy you meet. Sometimes you just have to live in the moment—step out and take a chance and see where it leads."

Liz shook her head. "Who are you and what have you done with my college roommate?"

"I know, I know. That doesn't sound like me. But that was the old me. Look at Purcell. Two days ago, I'd bet it never crossed his mind that he might not live to see the weekend. Maybe he was counting on visiting that cute girl at the corner store he'd been too chicken to ask out. And then, *poof*, the chance is gone. Forever."

"O-kay," Liz enunciated slowly, straining to decipher what Amy was trying to say.

Amy motioned toward Liz's private quarters. "Do you have time to sit for a minute?"

"Sure."

They settled into Liz's small living room, and Amy hugged a throw pillow to her chest. "I never told you how much I admired your gumption to give up the career you spent your life working toward, and a guy—who, by the way, really didn't want to let you go—to track down your mother's family. To rediscover who you are. And to make a new life for yourself."

"It's been an experience, that's for sure. But I can honestly say I haven't regretted a moment of it."

"Not even leaving Matt Sheridan?"

"Especially not leaving Matt." Just the thought of her last encounter with her ex made her skin crawl.

Amy's gaze drifted as if she were somewhere else in her mind.

"Has someone asked you to marry him?" Liz asked, noting that her friend's left ring finger was bare.

"What?" Amy's attention snapped back to Liz. "No. What would make you think that?"

"It's something that might scare the old you into running halfway across the country to your best friend's inn."

Amy's lips spread into a warm smile. "You're right, it probably would."

"So why are you really here?"

"I've spent my entire life living for the future."

"And now you're having a midlife crisis? Rethinking your priorities?"

The sparkle blinked out of Amy's eyes. "Midlife, no. Rethinking, yes."

An uneasy feeling swamped Liz. "Now you're scaring me."

"The truth is my future is *now*." The cheery lilt had returned to Amy's voice. "And I want to make the most of it."

Liz blinked hard, as Amy's earlier quips—*life's too short; carpe diem; live in the moment; my future is now*—echoed through her mind. "Are you sick?" Amy didn't look sick, a little thinner perhaps.

"Maybe. I don't know. I'm waiting on some test results."

Liz's heart stuttered. This didn't sound like any simple illness.

"But I can't remember ever feeling so free," Amy went on. "A whole lot of people have a lot less time than I might have—and they don't even know it. But one thing *I* know is that my job wasn't fulfilling me anymore. So I quit. And I plan to savor every moment I have left on this earth, whether that's one year or fifty."

Tears stinging her eyes, Liz swept Amy into a hug. They held each other for a long time as Liz mentally processed Amy's revelations. Then, sitting back on the couch, Liz pressed her for details.

Amy hugged her knees to her chest. "To be honest, my condition is the last thing I want to talk about. I think it would be way more exciting to track down John, don't you?" Suddenly straightening, she dropped her feet to the floor. "I'm sure I could still access my law firm's online search services," she said excitedly. "Let's see what we can turn up on his employment status, next of kin, and something that tells us where he might go or who might've had a beef with him."

Someone knocked twice. Mary Ann cracked open the door to Liz's private quarters. "Liz, you in here? This little beagle is looking for you."

Peanut wiggled through the opening and scampered across the floor to Liz, whimpering.

"I'm sorry, Peanut." Liz bent over and hugged the little fellow. "Don't you worry. I promise we'll find your owner." *If he doesn't end up in jail first.*

"You should let Peanut find him," Mary Ann suggested. "He's a tracker, right?"

Not a great one, if yesterday's competition was any indication, but... Liz shot Amy a skeptical look. It wouldn't be the first time Liz had used a dog to track someone. "It might be worth a try. What do you think?"

"It's a brilliant idea. Let's take him to the fields near where the body was found."

"Yeah, at the very least, we should be able to tell by Peanut's reactions if John had even been in the vicinity."

"Then let's go." Amy snatched up Peanut's leash from the end table. "Time to show us what you can really do, Peanut."

"Do you want to come along?" Liz asked Mary Ann.

"I can't this morning. Sadie and I are working on a project of our own that should help us get some answers."

"Really? What is it?" Liz asked.

Mary Ann's eyes twinkled. "A surprise. Go." She slipped out the door.

"I love how your friends always seem to be game to help you," Amy said, handing Peanut's leash to Liz as they followed Mary Ann to the foyer. "Hold this a second. I'll be right back." She sprinted up the stairs.

"I'll get Peanut harnessed in the car," Liz called up after her.

A few minutes later, Amy opened the passenger door and jumped inside. "Whatever Mary Ann and Sadie are up to, they're really enjoying themselves. I could hear them giggling as I came out."

"I can't imagine what the surprise is."

"The last time someone surprised me was you on my thirtieth birthday. I don't think my neighbors in my apartment building back in Boston even know my name." She shrugged. "Not that I've made an effort to get to know them."

Liz drove toward River Road. "Small communities are nice that way."

Peanut stuck his head out the window, his ears and tongue flopping in the wind.

"You know you're welcome to stay here as long as you like," Liz added.

Amy pressed her hand to her heart in dramatic actress style. "My very own Brigadoon."

Liz chuckled. "Not sure I can promise the romance part."

Amy tossed her a cheeky grin. "I can see you're a little rusty at picking up the cues."

Liz rolled her eyes.

The crime scene came into view. Liz stopped along the roadside and shifted the car into park. Peanut scratched frantically at the door.

"Okay, okay," Liz said. "Give me a second to come around and let you out. What's the word they use to tell a dog to track?" Liz asked Amy.

"I think John said he uses 'find.'" Amy handed Liz a ball cap. "It took some fast talking thanks to the chief's orders, but I convinced Sarah to let me into John's room so I could grab something for Peanut to go on. That's what I ran back for."

"Good thinking." Liz edged the rear door open and clasped Peanut's leash before he could take off. Holding him close, she held the hat to his nose. "Find, Peanut. Find."

The beagle squirmed to be put down. As soon as she set him on the ground, Peanut took off, baying, nose in the air instead of on the ground.

"I've heard of dogs that can pick up scents in the air," Amy shouted, chasing after Liz and Peanut.

His nose dropped to the ground around a section of depressed grass, where the body must've been found.

"With all the emergency personnel and investigators that have tromped around here," Liz said, "it'll be tough for Peanut to pick out John's scents from the others." What was she saying? She didn't *want* his scent to be here. Because that'd mean John had had something to do with Purcell's death. Or that he was a victim too.

"Maybe circle outside the trampled area," Amy suggested. "If John went off from here on foot, Peanut might pick up his scent that way."

Liz knelt beside the dog and held John's hat to his nose once more. "Find your master, Peanut. Find your master."

Peanut let out a single sharp bark and streaked for the bushes, almost pulling Liz off her feet. She was forced to let go of the leash and chase after him the best she could.

The dog crashed through the bushes, raced down the hill toward the river, and sniffed excitedly along the bank.

"I think he's on to something," Liz shouted back to Amy, who was picking her way down the hill at a more sedate pace.

A rabbit popped its head out of a hole along the bank and took off. The dog followed in hot pursuit, baying excitedly.

"No, Peanut. Stop," Liz called in her sternest voice.

The little dog skidded to a stop and sheepishly turned around, his ears drooping and his tail tucked between his legs.

"We're not hunting rabbits," Liz said, lightening her tone. She held the hat out to him again to sniff. "Find your master."

Peanut whined and didn't budge.

Liz nudged him. "Go on, find him."

Peanut took off again and this time managed to tree a squirrel.

Amy tramped up next to Liz, breathing heavily. "I'm afraid he isn't much of a tracker. I always heard beagles were naturals at it."

Peanut scrambled down the hill to the river and pounced at a frog. The frog hopped out of reach then disappeared under the water. Peanut started into the water, then seemed to change his mind and vigorously dug at the river's edge instead. After a minute, he directed a cocky "stay away!" bark at the hiding frog.

A boy's laugh punctuated the air.

Amy pointed across the river toward an adolescent Amish boy crouched in the grass on the hill. "Maybe he can help us."

"Excuse me," Liz called to him. "Did you—?"

The boy jumped up and scrambled over the hill. Liz caught a glimpse of an oddly colored patch on his elbow as he disappeared.

"Ah well," Amy said. "I thought if he was hanging round here today, he might have been here yesterday and might've seen what happened."

"It's possible. But even if we can figure out which home he came from, convincing his parents to let him answer our questions wouldn't be easy. The Amish don't like to get involved in English affairs."

"Sure, but you have an in, right?" Amy said, referring to Liz's relationships with her Amish cousins, thanks to her mom's former life here.

"I guess." Liz couldn't work up the same level of optimism. Liz's mom had left the Amish community long before Liz had been born, so even at the best of times some in the community looked at her a tad suspiciously. Not her close relatives, though, with whom she had a warm relationship. "I have a better idea." Liz called Peanut away from the river and herded him and Amy back to her car.

As Peanut jumped into the back seat, he spat out a small hunk of paper.

Liz snatched it up. She asked, "Where did you find this?" as if she expected him to answer. Her heart raced as she pried open the soggy corners of a memo-pad page.

"What does it say?" Amy asked.

"'Enjoy your . . . b . . .?'" Liz tilted the paper so Amy could see it. "I can't make it out. The writing is worse than my doctor's."

"'Enjoy your b—breakfast?'" Amy cocked her head, clearly struggling to decipher the rest. "'Bias equals bad judging. And bad judges need to go.'"

"Whoa." Liz stared at the crumpled page. "That sounds like a threat if I ever heard one. Did you see where Peanut picked this up?"

"Could've been when he ran through the bush. Or when he nuzzled the ground by the river."

"He barked after that, so he couldn't have had anything in his mouth."

"Good point. So it must've been as we were walking back up here. Or maybe when we were gawking at the boy on the other side of the river." Amy opened her door. "Who do you suppose wrote it?"

"Sounds like something a competitor could've written to Purcell."

"Yeah, but John? He didn't have a chance of winning, no matter who was judging." Amy scratched the window where Peanut's nose pressed against the glass. "No offense, Peanut."

"Somehow I doubt the chief will see it that way." Liz slipped inside the car.

"You're taking the note to the police station?"

Liz turned the car toward town. "There's somewhere else I'd like to stop first."

6

"Where are we going, Liz?" The curiosity in Amy's voice was unmistakable.

"The dog show," Liz replied. "I saw in the program we picked up that there was a breeders' breakfast yesterday morning," Liz went on. "I'm wondering if the judges were invited. I thought we could poke around and ask some questions about whether something happened there."

"Oh, good plan!" Amy squealed.

Liz's heart did an unexpected flip as she glanced at her friend—her possibly sick friend. They hadn't seen each other in years, yet they'd instantly slipped back into their comfortable camaraderie. Liz couldn't imagine life without her. "Are you sure?" she asked. "Because if you'd rather go sightseeing or something, I can—"

"No!" Amy's expression turned sheepish. "I mean, I don't want to sound morbid, because I know John's life might hang in the balance. But this sleuthing stuff is fun."

If a man weren't dead and her missing guest the prime suspect, Liz would've grinned at how very Nancy Drew they must seem. She parked in the fairgrounds lot.

"Uh-oh." Amy pointed to a pair of cruisers. "Looks like the police beat us to the punch."

"I imagine they're interviewing everyone who knew Purcell to find out if anyone had made death threats or something against him."

"Then we'll have to talk to people on the sly. We don't want them to babble to police that a couple of babes are walking around the place, asking the same questions."

Liz burst out laughing. "I don't think that's how they'd describe us. I'm pretty sure I've never earned that moniker, even when I was younger."

"Then you need glasses, girlfriend." Amy jumped out of the car and, opening the back door, grabbed Peanut's lead. "Because you clearly haven't seen the way Jackson looks at you."

Before Liz could counter her, an exuberant Peanut tugged Amy to the gate. Liz had a bad feeling he was thinking he'd find his owner here. To the female ticket taker at the gate, Liz casually said, "I wasn't sure if the event would go ahead after what happened last night."

"Things are a bit delayed, since police are interrogating everyone with a connection to the judge."

"Did you know him?" Liz asked.

"Not personally. But I can't say I'm surprised someone offed him. I sure wouldn't put it past a ribbon-hungry breeder to take whatever means necessary to eliminate bias." The woman leaned forward and added in a stage whisper, "I heard one of the judges took sick after the breeders' breakfast yesterday."

"Wow, I'd heard dog people took these shows seriously, but I had no idea it was that extreme."

The woman shrugged. "There are always a few bad eggs in every sport."

Amy pulled Liz aside. "I think we should start by hanging around the events Purcell was supposed to judge. Talk to the competitors and spectators. Get a feel for their sentiment toward the guy."

"We're here to get a lead on John, not on Purcell's killer."

"The two might be connected. Whoever killed Purcell might've been the last person to see John too."

"I see what you mean." And at the moment, the note Peanut had found was the only real clue they had. Liz dug the dog show program out of her purse and checked the schedule. "Purcell would've been judging conformation events right now in the east wing. Looks like he'd be working his way through the herding breeds."

"Let's go."

They found an especially talkative owner of a Pomeranian. "It's so sad. All the toy dog owners loved William Purcell. He understood our dogs like no other."

"I guess all the judges have their share of dissenters?"

The Pomeranian owner retied the bow in her dog's hair. "Yeah, but Mr. Purcell was the only one who got poisoned. He missed all his judging yesterday because of it."

"Poisoned?" Liz exchanged a telling glance with Amy. "I had no idea. Are you sure?"

"That's what everyone is saying now. Yesterday, they thought it was the flu. He got sick right after the breeders' breakfast."

Amy pulled Liz aside. "John wasn't at the breeders' breakfast. When he checked in, he told me he'd only just gotten to town."

"If we could figure out why Purcell called John in the afternoon, we might be able to convince the chief to start looking at John as a missing person instead of a suspect." Amy's expression morphed into her brow-crinkling, lawyer-getting-into-the-criminal's-mindset look. "Based on the note Peanut found, it seems clear whoever stabbed Purcell did it to finish off what the botched breakfast failed to accomplish." Amy scanned the competitors in the show ring—all owners of toy dogs. "The scrawl on that note was pretty distinctive. If we could get handwriting samples of everyone who was at the breakfast, we'd easily be able to match the culprit's to our note."

"Yeah, good luck with that. The culprit would see right through the ploy."

"Not necessarily. I might be able to come up with something he wouldn't expect. And when we get a handwriting match, we'll have our man."

"Or woman," Liz countered. "They say poison is the number-one weapon of choice for the fairer sex."

Amy dramatically clutched her throat. "Should I be warning your guests they'd better not get on your bad side?"

Liz's heart dipped.

It must've shown in her expression, because Amy frowned. "What is it?"

"Finding out who wrote the note and presumably poisoned Purcell's breakfast won't tell us why Purcell called John," Liz said.

"Good point. Maybe we're going about this all wrong. We should be asking people what they know about John." And Amy did just that with the very next person she met. Of course, they had to ask twenty-three people before they found one who even knew him. Or, at least, who recognized Peanut as John's dog.

"I remember he asked me if I knew William Purcell," the tall, bald border collie owner said. "But a lot of people were talking about the poor guy yesterday because of the way he took sick. It had more than a few people wondering if someone had spiked his OJ, if you know what I mean."

"Thank you," Amy said to the man and jerked Liz and Peanut behind a partition.

Liz tripped over Peanut and barely regained her balance to avoid face-planting on the floor. "What are you doing?"

Amy peeked around the corner of the partition. "The police chief was coming."

"So? We're not doing anything wrong. And I want to show him the note."

Amy hesitated. "You're right. If John was going around asking people about Purcell, he doesn't sound like someone who had a previous connection to him, let alone a motive to snuff him out."

Liz grimaced. She wanted to believe that for Amy's sake. But then that would also mean John's disappearance had nothing to do with

Purcell's death, and then they'd have zero leads on what happened to him.

A horrific screech sounded above the hum of the crowd.

People ducked and fled from the general direction of the sound. Without thinking, Liz raced toward the screamer.

"My dog," a distraught man wailed. And not just any man, it was Liz's guest, Edward. His adorable little shih tzu worriedly watched him, his tail jittering back and forth.

"What's wrong?" Liz asked.

Edward pointed to the dog's tail. "Someone snipped out a huge chunk of hair."

"Who?"

"I don't know," Edward seethed, his distress morphing to anger. "I only turned my back on him for a second."

Liz scanned the people who had begun to crowd back into the gap created by Edward's initial cry. She caught a glimpse of someone darting through the flow of people flocking in to see what was going on. The runner was of medium build, with a ball cap over his short hair. He was about five foot ten inches and wore a black bomber jacket. Liz started after him, but the crowd was too dense to get through. He disappeared around the corner, and by the time she reached it, he was nowhere in sight.

"Did you see someone run this way?" she asked at least half a dozen people, but they all shook their heads.

She surmised that the second he'd rounded the corner, he'd probably stopped running to avoid looking suspicious. Chances were the sabotage probably wasn't even connected to John's disappearance or to the other man's death. But it could've been. Maybe it'd been a diversion to throw off the police investigation.

Liz walked back to find Amy and Peanut, and spotted a lone Amish teen hovering at the fringes of the crowd gathered around Edward. Liz glanced at the boy's hands, looking for scissors and a clutch of dog hair. But his hands were stuffed in his coat pockets. Did she really think he'd get into such mischief?

Perhaps if there were a group of them enjoying their *Rumschpringe*—their chance to run wild—goading each other on, but there were no other Amish spectators in site. And they would be pretty easy to spot, in their plain clothes and bonnets or hats. Besides, if he were the culprit, he wouldn't hang around waiting to be caught, especially with how readily his wardrobe made him stand out in a crowd. But from how intensely he seemed to be watching the goings on, perhaps he'd seen something.

Liz circled toward him, and at the sight of a distinctively sewn patch at the elbow of his coat, her breath hitched. What were the chances more than one Amish boy would have the exact hand-sized patch on the exact same elbow? This was the same boy they'd seen watching them from the other side of the river. She hadn't gotten a good look at his features then, but the elbow patch gave him away.

"How unsportsmanlike," Amy declared to the bystanders. "Whoever did this ought to be ashamed to stoop to such tactics in the name of winning."

A murmur of agreement rose among the crowd.

Then the sea of people parted and Chief Houghton emerged. His gaze collided with Liz's, and his eyes darkened.

Liz shrank back at his uncharacteristic hostility. More than just a headache had to be behind it, and she wished she knew what. He couldn't be thinking she was harboring his supposed fugitive. Not when she was the one pressing him to find John.

"What's going on?" Stan directed the question at Liz.

Liz glanced across at the boy she'd been a mere ten feet from intercepting, but he'd disappeared. Again.

Amy answered the chief's question.

Stan turned to the crowd. "Did anyone see who did this?"

The crowd dispersed, shaking their heads.

"I saw someone hurrying away, when everyone else was coming to see what the ruckus was about," Liz said. She gave the chief the runner's description.

Stan scribbled it into his notepad, nodding. "And what are you doing here?" he asked, his tone a tad more friendly than the dark look he'd first thrown her.

"Peanut was supposed to compete in the dog show," Amy jumped in. "So we came hoping to find someone who might know John and where he could have gotten to."

Stan's eyebrow arched. "And?"

She shrugged. "No one seems to know him."

"But," Liz interjected, "we also took Peanut to where you found Purcell's body because we figured if John had been there his dog should pick up his scent."

Stan looked intrigued by the notion. "Did he?"

"No, but he did find this." Liz handed him the note Peanut had found. "We're not sure where exactly, because he ventured a little far afield. But if Purcell had been carrying the note and dropped it, the wind could've caught hold of it too."

The chief studied the still damp piece of paper.

"I'm sure you've already discovered Purcell's breakfast was poisoned yesterday morning," Liz ventured.

Stan's brow furrowed. "Who told you that?"

Liz did a double take. How could he have not heard? "Several people have mentioned it."

"Purcell told staff he had a flu bug."

"Did the coroner check his blood for poison?"

The chief's jaw worked back and forth. "Of course."

"And?"

The chief scrutinized Edward's shih tzu before responding. "You and your friend and that dog should go home." Chief Houghton tucked the note they'd handed over into his inside coat pocket. "Thanks for this."

"John couldn't have poisoned Purcell," Liz insisted.

"He didn't even get to town until after the breakfast yesterday," Amy added.

Stan nodded and then told Edward he was sorry about his dog, but there was nothing he could do.

As the chief started to walk away, Amy blurted, "You're trying to pin this on the wrong—"

Liz squeezed her arm. "The chief knows what he's doing." And if Amy hadn't let herself get attached to John so quickly, the lawyer in her would see the flaws in her defense of the man. But it didn't explain why Stan was freezing Liz out. Unless . . .

Maybe he was afraid her infatuated lawyer friend might use whatever information they gleaned from the investigation to help John escape charges.

7

Liz and Amy returned to the inn in silence. In her gut, Liz didn't think John was a murderer any more than Amy did. But there was plenty to be suspicious about, and Amy wasn't ready to go there.

Inside the door, Amy unhooked Peanut's leash from his collar, and the dog scampered over to Beans, who hadn't even bothered to get up from his rug to welcome them home.

Sadie appeared at Sew Welcome's entrance off the rotunda, waving a flash drive. "I brought some pictures from the dog show for you to add to the inn's website."

Mary Ann bustled up beside her. "Never mind that now. Did Peanut find anything?"

Liz filled them in on the morning's excitement, from the note Peanut found at the crime scene to their run-in with the chief at the dog show after Edward's dog's fur was maliciously clipped.

Sadie seemed to be mulling over Liz's account of what happened there. "It certainly sounds as if a disgruntled competitor knocked off the poor judge," she said. "Probably the same one who snipped—what kind of dog was it again?"

"A shih tzu."

"Right. The same one who snipped the shih tzu's fur. I'm surprised Chief Houghton dismissed the incident. It's difficult to imagine more than one success-crazed competitor in the bunch."

"I agree. I can't believe he didn't even try to find the culprit," Mary Ann said. "The guy had to have still been carrying the scissors."

"I don't know," Amy said. "The guy would have to be pretty brazen to risk getting caught for something as silly as snipping hair after getting away with stabbing a judge."

"You don't think it was the same person then?" Sadie asked.

"Oh, it's possible. In my line of work, I've seen all types of criminals. Most aren't terribly bright. At least the ones who get caught aren't."

"You're not going to let the chief stop you from snooping around the dog show anymore, are you?" Mary Ann asked Liz. "Seems as if that's where you're most likely to get a lead on your missing guest."

Liz motioned toward the library. "I thought we'd see what we can find out about him online. Perhaps we can track down his employer or family. A colleague or family member is bound to have some idea where he might be."

"Nonsense," Sadie said. "That's the first thing the police would've done. I was thinking if you went to the dog show as a competitor, instead of just a spectator, you could snoop behind the scenes too. Maybe pick up some whisperings you'd miss otherwise."

"I think we should leave the investigation to the police," Liz said, backing toward library. Yes, she felt like a hypocrite, but at the sudden mental image of Sadie posing as a dog show competitor, Liz had a new appreciation for why the chief had been so insistent about her not investigating. "Besides, Peanut isn't my dog. I don't think they'll let me stand in as a proxy. I wouldn't even know what to do."

"Oh, no, I was thinking with Beans," Sadie said.

Liz had taken a sip from her water bottle and nearly sprayed a little out in a burst of laughter. "There's no way anyone would believe it. I don't think Beans knows how to stand for conformation. I don't even know if he's registered."

"It's a good idea though," Amy chimed in. "I saw some open classes in the program—an obedience one and an agility one. Any registered dog can compete in those, and there's no special stance or body type for it."

"And he *is* registered. Beans is of noble stock," Sadie informed her haughtily.

Liz couldn't stop laughing, picturing Beans in such a high-end event. "I'm sorry. I adore Beans, but he's the laziest dog on the planet. I can't see him waddling between the spikes on an agility course, let alone scampering up a seesaw or jumping over rails."

"There's—" Mary Ann began, but Sadie stopped her and whispered feverishly in her ear, then turned to Liz.

"Did you talk to that woman who was so mad at your guest?" Sadie asked.

Liz's pulse jumped. "No. Not yet." Between the chief's suspicions about John, and Amy's bombshell about her health immediately after the chief left, and then taking Peanut out to track John and following up on the note Peanut had found, thoughts of Rhonda Piper had completely slipped her mind. And Rhonda clearly knew John.

Liz recalled Stan's theory that John had chosen to disappear.

If it were true, Rhonda would likely enjoy nothing better than getting him in trouble by spilling everything she knew about him. She no doubt thought John was more than capable of killing Purcell. And with any luck, something she had to say would help them figure out where he could be.

Liz glanced out the window to the parking area. "Her car's gone. She must've headed over to the dog show too."

"All the more reason why you should go back," Mary Ann said.

"Well, let's do the computer search and grab some lunch before we return," Amy suggested. "Maybe by then the chief will be gone."

As Liz entered the library, she fought a compulsion to race straight back to the show and find Rhonda—the one and only person she'd met who had seemed to know John before his visit to Pleasant Creek.

Amy fetched her own laptop so they could double their effort. "I'll access my firm's services, while you see what you can turn up on him online."

Liz didn't ask how she still had access if she'd quit her job. If she was sneaking in a back door she shouldn't be, Liz didn't want to know.

A ridiculously high number of John Baxters lived in Indiana, but when Liz used the town name he'd scrawled into her register to narrow the search, the number dropped to nothing. She tried reverse lookup on his phone number, but it came up as an unidentified cell phone user. On a whim she plugged the entire address he'd given her into a geography app. "No way. He'd like us to believe he lives in the middle of a quarry. I've got to say his paying cash is not looking all that innocent."

Amy glanced up from her computer. "You sound like you're starting to believe he's guilty."

Liz raked her fingers through her hair. "I don't know what to think. It looks as if his phone was a burner phone. But if he came here intending to kill Purcell, why on earth would he bring Peanut, only to abandon him?"

"Yeah, it doesn't make sense. And clearly your instincts are telling you he's not a killer."

Peanut must've heard his name, because he came racing into the room and launched himself into Liz's lap.

She chuckled at the dog's exuberant kisses. "No one would leave such a friendly fellow of his own free will, would he?" she cooed. "How about you? You find anything?"

"Unfortunately my password doesn't work anymore on the paid search services I was hoping to use. And without an address or birthdate or employer or even a former alma mater, it's tough to zero in on any useful information."

Liz's finger caught in Peanut's collar as she set him down. "Ooh, hold on a second there, boy." She freed her finger and scrutinized the metal dog tag. "Why didn't I think to look at this before? Maybe we can get something from his dog license number."

"Perfect." Amy grabbed a pencil. "What is it?"

Liz let out a frustrated sigh. "He's not wearing a dog license tag, just a name tag with his owner's phone number." Liz squinted at the number. "Only it isn't John's number. At least not his cell phone number."

"Maybe it's his home phone. We can do reverse lookup on it and get an address."

Liz read off the number as Amy typed it into a search.

"The exchange is from the Indianapolis area, but I can't get an ID."

Liz snatched up her phone and dialed the number.

The call went to voice mail and a female voice said, "This is Trish and Bob's. Leave a message."

"You're kidding me." Liz hung up without leaving a message. "The number wasn't John's." Liz scrutinized the tag to make sure she had dialed correctly. "I suppose it could've been misprinted."

"Or it's an old number somebody else has now."

Liz ground her teeth, knowing Amy wouldn't like the third option.

"What?"

"Maybe Peanut doesn't even belong to John," Liz said softly.

"Why didn't you leave a message?" Amy asked. "That's the only way we're going to find out."

Liz shook her head and hit redial. "I was too surprised. I wasn't thinking." She waited for the voice mail recording to replay, then left the inn's number and said she was calling about a beagle named Peanut.

Liz shut down her computer. "We should head back to the dog show. Finding Rhonda is the only good lead we have. I wonder if John begged, borrowed, or stole Peanut with ulterior motives to get behind the scenes at the dog show, just like Sadie suggested I do with Beans." Only Liz had a bad feeling John hadn't merely been looking for information. "And we need to figure out why."

"One second." Amy raised a finger to urge Liz to wait. "I'm doing a search on William Purcell to see if we can figure out his connection to John."

There were numerous media articles on the man since he was a dog show judge. "He was born in Florida and only recently moved to Indiana. His wife died five or six years ago in childbirth."

"Oh, wow, the poor man."

"And look at this." Amy pointed to the paragraph in the online article she was reading. "Two years ago, a breeder backed into him in the parking lot outside a dog show. He claimed it was an accident and he wasn't charged, but it was apparently no secret among the dog show community that the man had a serious beef with Purcell's judging. Sounds as if we need to run with my idea to collect handwriting samples to find this guy."

Liz shook her head. "How are we supposed to convince people to write something for us?"

"We could pretend we're doing a survey."

"Most people would balk at that. I sure would."

Amy's face brightened and she snapped her fingers. "I've got an idea."

"What?"

"Give me fifteen minutes and I'll show you."

Liz held her hands up in surrender. "Okay, you get your plan ready. I need to find Sarah and let her know Peanut's owner might call. And to ask her to keep an eye on him for me."

"I'll bag some of your yummy muffins to take along for our lunch too."

Liz found Sarah changing the sheets on Rhonda's bed, in an unexpectedly empty room. "Rhonda left?"

"*Ja.* Didn't you check her out? Her bags were gone when I came in to clean."

"No. I'll give her a call." Liz retreated to the library and looked up the phone number and address Rhonda supplied when she checked in. The phone number went to voice mail. Liz explained about seeing that she'd left with her luggage and asked if she wished to be checked out. She left her cell phone number and asked for a call back.

There was no need to tell her she also had some questions about John.

John's argument with Rhonda flashed through her mind, and a more sobering thought struck her. What if Rhonda was the one who had stolen the corn knife? She certainly seemed to hate John enough to do something rash. Liz had no idea if she knew Purcell, but maybe he hadn't been the intended target. He could've simply been in the wrong place at the wrong time.

Liz fished the master key from her pocket and hurried up to John's room for a closer look. Trepidation rattled her stomach as she twisted the key in the lock. *The chief said not to clean the room—he didn't say I couldn't look.*

She felt inside the pockets of John's clothes, but came up empty-handed. She checked his shaving kit, hoping to score a pill bottle with his pharmacist's address on it. Nothing.

She returned to the closet. Something wasn't right, but she couldn't quite put her finger on it. She looked down at her pants, covered in hair courtesy of the exuberant Peanut, and then back at the immaculate slacks hanging in the closet. Even a dog owner's freshly laundered clothes would still have traces of dog hair, unless John was so obsessive-compulsive that he took a lint brush to every item of clothing before he packed. Liz groaned. Amy wasn't going to like it, but this convinced Liz that phone number on Peanut's collar was no misprint or old number—Peanut didn't belong to John.

The stairs creaked and she quickly let herself out and locked the door behind her. Gloria's chow chow sat at the top of the stairs, watching Gloria climb them.

"Back so soon?" Liz asked the woman.

"Yes, we only had one event today." Gloria held up a blue ribbon and grinned. "It went well."

"You won? Congratulations!"

Her grin widened, then quickly reverted to a more dignified smile. "Thank you."

Liz chuckled. Gloria Hunt might be all prim and proper on the outside, but inside she was as giddy as a schoolgirl.

Amy arrived in the foyer at the same time as Liz. In one hand she held a bag of muffins. In the other was a bright-yellow poster board decorated in the corners with colorfully drawn flowers. "Your Material Girls said we could use this to collect condolence messages to try—"

Liz shook her head.

"Don't give me that look," Amy scolded. "This could work. I know what you're thinking—our culprit will just decline signing. But if he's smart, he wouldn't want to draw attention to himself by doing that. Don't you think?"

"I think we might have another suspect in Purcell's murder or at least John's disappearance."

"Who?"

"Rhonda Piper. She had reservations to stay through the weekend, but she cleared out this morning, without even bothering to officially check out."

"Sounds like someone on the run."

"Yeah, that's what I'm afraid of."

"You think she attacked John?"

"She certainly seemed to hate him enough to be able to. I need to tell the chief."

A muscle in Amy's jaw flexed as if she didn't like the idea. "How about we wait to see if we spot her or even her car at the dog show first?

Could be she just got it into her head she didn't want to sleep under the same roof as John. It wasn't as if his disappearance was on the news this morning. We could be reading more into her leaving than there is."

"You think so?"

Amy contemplatively tapped her fingers to her lips. "I don't know. Running makes her look guiltier—not what a smart criminal would do. But like I said, they're rarely smart."

Liz tried Rhonda's number again. But once more, it went to voice mail. The low rumble in the background of the recording reminded Liz of the background sounds during her conversation with the guy who answered John's phone. "He must've been near a train crossing."

"Who was near a train crossing?" Amy asked.

"The teenager on John's phone last night. I heard a train whistle and the rattle of a train passing."

"What time was that?" asked Mary Ann, who'd meandered into the room.

Liz pulled up the call log on her phone. "10:03."

"That'd be the nightly freight train. It blows its whistle at two crossings and you can pretty much set your watch by them. One's a couple of minutes before ten. The other is a few minutes after."

"This is great," Liz said. "Maybe we can find this kid yet."

"Except we don't know the teen was even in Pleasant Creek," Amy reminded her.

"We know he was close enough that my call was picked up by the cell tower on the edge of town. I also heard voices in the background and country music."

"There's a bar and restaurant, the Grill House, that has a regular country music band near the train crossing on the south end of town," Mary Ann said.

"Is that near where they found Purcell?" Amy asked.

"It's next to the Shady Rest Motel," Mary Ann said. "Do you think your guest would've holed up there?"

Liz bit her lip, not liking that prospect. After all, if he was innocent, why not return to the inn? "We should check it out."

"Check what out?" Sadie asked, joining them.

Liz explained.

"Are you planning to go straight to the dog show from there?" Mary Ann asked. At Liz's nod, she whistled toward their shop. "Then we'll come too."

"Okay," Liz said. Before she could ask what the whistle was for, Beans waddled out of the shop, looking fluffier—and grumpier—than Liz had ever seen him. "Oh my."

"Doesn't he look wonderful?" Sadie gushed. "We made him an adorable costume for the Christmas Costume Open Class Parade."

"The surprise you mentioned?" Liz injected as much enthusiasm in her voice as she could muster.

Mary Ann grinned. "The parade is open to all types of dogs of all ages." She scratched Beans's chin, smiling. "He just has to look cute."

"And we've already paid his entry fee." Sadie handed Liz the paperwork to prove it.

"But the parade isn't until tomorrow," Mary Ann said, "so I'm not sure how that works with being allowed to access the competitors' tents today."

"There is an open class in the obedience event this afternoon," Sadie said. "You know he won't go chasing after anything they might let loose in the field to tempt the dogs. He's much too dignified for that."

Dignified is not the word I would have chosen. Liz stared at the entry form, shaking her head.

Amy giggled. "Let's take him. It'll be fun."

"I guess it couldn't hurt." But even as Liz said it, a dark foreboding crept over her.

8

Liz pulled into the back parking lot of the Shady Rest Motel, not sure what she expected to find. If she went into the Grill House and asked the restaurant staff if they'd noticed a teenager talking on a cell phone at about ten p.m., they'd look at her as if she'd lost her marbles. What kid didn't have his ear or his thumbs glued to a phone these days?

"We should check out the garbage," Sadie suggested. "If your Mr. Baxter was mugged, maybe whoever attacked him tossed whatever he didn't want to keep."

Or John tossed his cell phone so he couldn't be tracked. Liz shook the thought from her head. Things weren't always what they seemed.

"Give me a boost," Sadie said to Mary Ann, gripping the top rim of the Dumpster. The woman was in her seventies, but she never let that stop her.

"Wait. Let me have a look," Liz volunteered. She stepped up on the metal outcropping meant for the collection trucks spikes and peeked over the top. "It's empty. Must've been dumped this morning."

"But look at what Beans found." Amy crouched beside the dog and coaxed a pen from his mouth. "It has your logo on it, Liz."

Liz's stomach somersaulted.

"Did John pocket one of your pens?" Sadie asked.

Liz left a pen and small notepad in each guest room. Her mind skittered back to her earlier search of John's room. "He might have. The notepad and pen weren't in his room, now that I think about it."

Amy scanned the motel and Grill House parking lots. "His car's not here." She headed toward the front of the motel.

"Where are you going?"

"To see if he checked in here last night."

Liz wasn't sure which was worse—to think he was alive and on the run, or that he'd been attacked and left for dead somewhere. No—it was definitely worse to think he was dead.

Mary Ann picked up a hunk of gold plastic from the parking lot. "Looks as if someone had one of the parking lights on the side of their car smacked."

"I'll be right back." Liz strode toward the Grill House.

A young female hostess in black jeans and a black T-shirt greeted Liz at the door.

Liz declined a seat. "I'm actually looking for someone who I think might've been here last night. Did you have a large group of high school or college kids here?"

"Yes."

"Do you happen to know the names of any of them? I think one of them found my guest's phone and I'm trying to track him down."

"No, sorry. I'm new around here. I don't know many people."

"Is there anyone else in who worked last night who might be able to help me?"

The hostess pressed her lips together and glanced toward the kitchen. "I doubt it."

"Okay. Thanks anyway." She'd known it would be a long shot. Liz reached for the door and another idea struck her. She quickly brought the Internet up on her smartphone and did an image search for Rhonda Piper. Images of her guest along with images of a few other Rhonda Pipers filled her screen. She zoomed in on one of her guest and turned it toward the hostess. "Was this woman here last night?"

The hostess studied the photo, then shook her head. "Not that I recall."

Unfortunately, when Liz tried the same method to pull up a picture of John, no pictures of him came up. "I'll be right back." Liz hurried out and flagged down Sadie, who was still scanning the ground around the Dumpster for more clues. "Do you still have the pictures from yesterday on your camera?"

"Yep." Sadie lifted it from where it hung against her torso and tapped a few buttons. "You want one of John?"

"Yes. Do you have one?"

"Sure do." She took the camera off and handed it to Liz, screen up. "Here's a good one."

"Thanks, I'll be right back." Liz showed the picture to the restaurant hostess, but she didn't remember John from the night before either.

"Sorry."

"I'm not," Liz admitted.

Amy had returned to the car by the time Liz reemerged. "Any luck?" Liz asked.

"No," Amy said dejectedly. "The receptionist refused to tell me one way or the other. Client privacy and all."

"Well, this isn't getting us anywhere," Liz said. "We might as well go to the dog show and see if we can use your crazy scheme to collect some handwriting samples."

They all piled back into the vehicle. Fifteen minutes later, they pulled into the parking lot at the dog show.

"Goodie," Sadie said. "The coast is clear."

"Huh?" Liz glanced out the car window, trying to figure out what she was talking about.

"No police cars."

Amy chuckled and then whispered to Liz, "Your friends are such a hoot. I love them."

A warm feeling marshmallowed over the anxiety that'd been churning Liz's insides since yesterday evening. She supposed she took for granted that she knew she could always count on the Material Girls to be there for her. And Jackson too. It was something Amy must have acutely realized was missing in her own life when she got her possible diagnosis. Liz promised herself she'd be there for Amy too, whatever it took.

"Coming?" Sadie asked.

Everyone, including Beans, stood in the parking lot, waiting for Liz to climb out of the car.

She jumped out, and Sadie snatched the entry forms Liz had left tucked between the seats. "You'll need these. If you hurry, you'll have just enough time to get Beans into the obedience trial."

"I don't know about this," Liz protested.

Amy laughed. "What are you afraid of? If he does terrible, he does terrible. You're not actually trying to compete. It's not a big deal."

True. And Liz didn't care if people snickered at them, since the whole show could probably use a bit of levity around now, but . . . "Do I really want to draw that much attention to myself, if I'm supposed to be quietly snooping?" she reasoned. "Because when Beans goofs up, he does it in a big way."

Sadie brushed away the concern with a sweep of her arm. "You'll be fine."

Liz checked Beans in and meandered through the tents that had been off-limits to her the day before. Several competitors were fixing up their dogs' hairdos.

"Oh, what an adorable bulldog," a woman in her mid-thirties said to Liz. Her dog sat perfectly poised at her side, while Beans plopped down beside Liz and scratched. "Hi," the woman added, extending her hand. "I'm Susan."

"Your spaniel is adorable too," Liz said, after introducing herself and Beans.

"Schnauzer."

"Oops, sorry. I'm new to this, so I'm not really up on all the breeds. We're just trying it out and seeing how he does."

"Perfectly all right. Refreshing to see someone out for fun." She glanced at another competitor who was berating a guy because his dog had left a streak of white fur on her otherwise immaculate black dress pants. "Clearly some people take the show far too seriously."

"I see what you mean."

With a flick of her fingers, she dismissed the other woman, who was now savagely whacking at her pants with a lint roller. "That's nothing compared to the other incidents."

"You mean the shih tzu that had his tail hairs snipped?"

"That and yesterday, one of the schnauzers had a bowlful of burrs rubbed into his fur."

"Ouch." How could someone be so cruel to an innocent animal?

"Yes, the poor thing winced every time one was pulled off. Everyone knows that one of the other competitors must have done it."

"It sounds as if different competitors are behind the incidents, since the schnauzer and the shih tzu wouldn't compete against each other, would they? Aren't they in different groups?"

"If they won their own conformation classes and groups, they'd go head-to-head for best in show. And then there's the judge who was killed. It's enough to give all dog show competitors a bad name." The woman squeezed Liz's arm. "I'm sorry. Listen to me go on. You don't need to hear this. Just go out there and have fun."

Liz smiled. "Thank you. Sounds like you've been doing this a long time."

"Oh yes, my parents are breeders. I've been hanging around these events as long as I can remember."

"I'd heard some of the breeders didn't think much of the judge who died."

"Sadly, that could be said of most of the large dog breeders. A couple of highly competitive ones like Philip Rutherford and Alex Caldwell had even started a petition to try and convince event organizers to stop bringing Purcell in. But the small dog owners love him."

Beans tugged at his leash and whined.

"It's okay, boy," Liz said. "We'll be going in the ring soon."

Susan grinned. "I think he's more interested in that cute border collie over there. And if I'm not mistaken, she's from one of Philip Rutherford's litters."

"Really?" Philip sounded like a breeder they definitely wanted a writing sample from. "Can you see him?"

Susan rose up onto her tiptoes and scanned the crowds around the ring. "Not at the moment, but he'll be at the agility trial after this one, I'm sure. You can't miss him. He's six foot three and balder than a bowling ball."

Big and bald, and breeds border collies? Could Rutherford be the competitor who'd wowed audiences at the tracking trial—the one she'd seen John chatting with afterward?

The announcer invited all entrants in the Open Obedience Trial to enter the ring.

"That's us," Liz said. "See you around."

"Good luck."

Liz gave the leash a short tug and trotted into the ring behind the border collie and her owner. To her surprise, Beans heeled perfectly, and when the judge said, "Stop," Beans obeyed before Liz said a word. He sat tight to her left side, his head high, but while he pretended to be giving Liz his attention, his eyes kept darting in the cute border collie's direction.

"Are you smitten?" Liz whispered to him.

From the sidelines, Liz could see Sadie and Mary Ann miming wild cheers, their grins as wide as could be.

Liz grinned back, as Beans obeyed the command to lie down. Of course, that had always been his favorite, so he was an expert.

When the judge asked entrants to instruct their dogs to roll over, Liz glanced worriedly at Sadie. Beans was so overweight, she wasn't sure he was even capable of rolling. She mimicked the hand signal other competitors were using and said quietly, "Roll over, Beans, for your girlfriend."

Beans glanced at the border collie and mimicked her roll, although not nearly as gracefully.

"Way to go, Beans," Liz whispered. "Boy, have I been underestimating you."

His tongue lolled and he gave her a doggy grin.

He executed each of the remaining commands with equal enthusiasm, followed by a little shoulder check to see if his newfound crush was watching. Which she certainly seemed to be.

At the end, he strutted out of the ring, sporting a third-place ribbon more proudly than the first-place winner, as Mary Ann and Sadie did a wild jig on the sidelines. "That's our boy!"

But much to Liz's—and Beans's—chagrin, the border collie and her owner slipped through the crowd before Liz could introduce herself and her surprising bulldog. Mary Ann and Sadie fussed over Beans enough to make up for it though.

"You two were terrific out there," Amy said. "I'm afraid I haven't had any success. I haven't spotted Rhonda anywhere. Although I did find one person who talked to her yesterday. Turns out Rhonda's taking a degree in animal behavior and is here to interview subjects. At least, that's the story she gave the woman who spoke with me."

"Huh. You'd think she would've been more interested in talking to my guests about their animals then, instead of laying into John."

"Yup. Could've just been a cover story for whatever her real reason was for being here. But the woman said Rhonda spent a good twenty minutes asking her about her dog's behavior."

"Hmm."

Amy held up the poster board she'd brought to collect condolences for Purcell's family. "I've collected more than forty condolences so far, but none with handwriting that looks like what was on the note Peanut found."

"Do you have one from a Philip Rutherford or Alex Caldwell?"

Amy scanned the card. "Nope."

"I think we should ask them. A woman told me they started a petition to try to keep Purcell from judging. She said we'd find Philip at the agility ring. He's a big, bald guy."

They all meandered in that direction. Sadie was the first to spot him. "There!" She pointed to the current competitor running his dog through the course.

Amy nodded. "Could be."

As he finished the course, the announcer gave his name and time, confirming their hopes. The announcer added this was Rutherford's fortieth year competing.

"Let's go." Amy hurried over to him. "Excuse me, Mr. Rutherford," she called out. "We're collecting condolences from entrants for Judge Purcell's family. Having a word from someone who's been participating at these shows for as many years as you have would mean a lot to them, I'm sure."

Liz didn't miss the distasteful look Rutherford quickly masked.

"I'd be happy to." He accepted the pen from Amy and then read a few of the sentiments already shared. Finally he wrote a couple lines of his own. He gave them a forced smile and walked away.

Amy excitedly drew Liz behind a partition, out of the man's line of sight if he turned around, and then pointed to his nearly indecipherable scrawl. "I'm no expert, but it sure looks the same to me."

"Oh, yeah. All his round letters have that same flattened look as in the note Peanut found."

"And the *b*'s lean the same wrong way, because he's a lefty. He's got to be our guy."

Pulling out her phone, Liz exchanged a glance with Amy. "Stay put," she mouthed, the chief's warning not to investigate John echoing in her head. After all, if Rutherford were the murderer, he wouldn't stand around and let two women he could squash like bananas accuse him in front of a crowd of witnesses. Then again, the crowd might offer them some protection. Not that it had helped protect Edward's shih tzu or that schnauzer.

When the chief picked up, Liz snuck a peek around the corner of the partition to ensure Rutherford was still out of earshot. Mary Ann and Sadie stood rooted, looking as if they were both holding their breath, their gazes bouncing from Amy to Rutherford to Liz.

She turned her back to them and spoke quietly into the phone. "I think we've identified who wrote that note Peanut found."

"Do I want to know how?" Resignation tinged the chief's voice.

"We've been collecting condolences on a big card for William Purcell's family. We think we have a match on the handwriting."

His grunt sounded begrudgingly impressed. "Where are you now?"

"The dog show." Liz hated how her heart thumped. Sure he'd told her to go home. But it wasn't as if she'd set out to defy him.

"All right. I'd better see what you have. Meet me at the front entrance in ten minutes."

"Will do." Liz's heart lightened. It felt as if they were finally on the same team again. "And don't worry. I have no intention of confronting him."

"Glad to hear it."

Liz ended the call—only to find Amy making small talk with Rutherford. At the word *breakfast*, trepidation punched through Liz's chest. Her bold friend might be reckless enough to attempt to goad a confession out of him.

9

Liz planted herself behind Rutherford and silently sliced her hand across her throat to signal to Amy to cut short the questions.

Amy ignored her.

Liz shifted until she caught Amy's gaze and then jerked her head toward the concession area. "Let's eat," she said loudly.

Amy's teeth gritted. She said one last thing to Rutherford, still sporting a semblance of a smile, then rejoined Liz, Mary Ann, and Sadie. "I think I could've gotten him to confess," she hissed to Liz.

Liz steered her away from the show ring. "You can take the girl out of the courtroom, but you can't take the lawyer out of the girl. We're meeting the chief at the entrance."

Amy grinned. She really seemed to be enjoying the chase.

Mary Ann and Sadie fell into step beside them, looking equally pleased.

Liz might have felt the same if Purcell's killer hadn't used her corn knife, and if they knew where John was. Liz furrowed her brow, an uncomfortable inconsistency striking her. "How'd Rutherford get hold of my corn knife? If he's the killer. I never saw him at the inn. And he's the kind of guy you don't miss."

"Maybe he stopped in when we were all at the dog show," Sadie said.

"But we saw him there." Liz countered. "And it's not as if he knew I'd left a corn knife lying around."

"You're right," Mary Ann said. "He must have an accomplice. Like one of your guests."

Liz sighed. So they were back to suspecting John again. Or maybe Rhonda.

Looking ahead, she saw that Chief Houghton stood at the entrance, scanning the crowd. He visibly relaxed when he spotted Liz and the girls heading his way. "Who do you think wrote the note?" he asked. His gaze dropped to Beans, who sat at Liz's feet, looking almost prim and proper. Well, as prim and proper as a wrinkled bulldog could look.

The chief rolled his eyes.

Amy handed him the sympathy poster.

"Amy had this brilliant idea of collecting condolences for the victim's family," Sadie said.

"And Philip Rutherford's scrawl"—Amy pointed it out to him— "matches the handwriting on the note. Don't you think?"

The chief pulled a clear evidence bag that contained the note from the inside pocket of his jacket and compared the writing to that on the card. "Hmm, it does look remarkably similar."

"So are you going to arrest him?" Sadie prodded.

"I have no grounds. Even if this proved he wrote the note, I have no evidence he hurt Purcell."

"But if you put the screws to him," Sadie pressed, "I know you could break him."

A grin tugged at the chief's lips. "I appreciate the vote of confidence. Where's Rutherford now?"

"His dog just finished the agility course," Liz said. "I imagine he'll hang around there until the awards are given." Liz gave a description, adding, "He has a border collie with him. He breeds them."

"And he was at the breeders' breakfast," Amy chimed in. "He told me."

"Find out if he's staying at the Shady Rest Motel," Sadie said. "Beans found one of Liz's pens in its parking lot. It might help place Rutherford at her inn or spook him enough to spill who he's working with."

That brought a confused look to the chief's face.

"I think the guy who answered John's phone last night might've been in that area," said Liz. "Remember the sounds I told you I heard in the background? Well, the motel is near a train crossing and a bar or restaurant that features a country music band."

"Yeah," Mary Ann said, "so we're thinking this Rutherford fellow tossed John's phone in the Dumpster behind his hotel. Only maybe the kid saw him and retrieved it."

Stan gave Liz a questioning look.

"We don't know how or if he's connected to John. Although I'm pretty sure Rutherford didn't visit my inn himself and snatch my corn knife." Liz filled him in on Rhonda's suspicious hasty departure that morning as well, and their accomplice theory. "Hopefully Rutherford can tell you where they are."

Stan nodded. "Go home, ladies. And this time, stay there. Oh, and Liz?" He paused until she met his gaze. "Good work."

She beamed.

"Let's go, girls," Amy said brightly, herding them out the door. "Our work here is done."

Sadie glanced up from her camera's screen with a grin. "I think I may have a lead on someone else you should talk to." She zoomed in on something, then turned the screen toward Liz. "Is this the teenager you saw earlier today?" The face of an Amish adolescent filled the screen.

"Yes."

Sadie zoomed out to show that he'd been in the crowd during the agility competition. Then she flicked through more photos and stopped again, zoomed in. "Here he is again, right?"

Liz nodded.

Sadie zoomed out to show the picture was from the day before. The boy had been among the spectators watching the tracking competition—the one John had competed in. "There's more," Sadie said, bringing up a picture of the concession area. This time the boy appeared to be watching people.

"What day was that?" Liz asked.

"Yesterday. He looks like an observant type. He may have seen something important without even realizing it."

"Woohoo!" Amy cheered. "We make a super-sleuthing team."

Liz wasn't so optimistic. "If he's even still here, he'll just bolt again as soon as he sees us."

"So you talk to him at home," Sadie said.

"We don't know who he is, let alone where he lives," Liz countered.

Sadie started for the car. "The Amish community isn't that big, and I daresay the number who'd attend a dog show is even smaller. Sarah might be able to identify him for us."

"If he did see anything, the elders might not want him to talk," Liz said.

Mary Ann nudged her. "I'm sure you can convince him."

Liz held her peace on the way back to the inn, not wanting to dash their hopes.

As was not uncommon, thanks to Sadie and Mary Ann's fabric and notions store being inside, an Amish buggy was parked in front of the inn when Liz drove in.

"I think that's Miriam's buggy," Mary Ann said. "I recognize her quilt on the seat."

"Perfect," Sadie said. "If Sarah can't ID our boy, Miriam might be willing to help."

"Why's that?" Amy asked. "Is she one of the relatives?"

"My cousin," Liz said.

"And a good friend," Mary Ann added.

They all tromped inside to Sarah's bright, "Oh, there they are now."

Liz let Beans off his leash, much to Peanut's delight, then gave Miriam a hug as the dogs romped off together.

Miriam turned her warm smile to Sadie and Mary Ann. "Perfect timing. I ran out of thread. I'd almost given up hope of getting some today when I saw the store was closed and Sarah said you went to the *Hund* show."

"I'm so sorry to have inconvenienced you." Mary Ann rushed to unlock the shop door.

Sadie, for her part, sidled up to Miriam with her camera. "Look who else was at the dog show. Do you know him?"

Miriam looked at the picture. "Yes. That's young Joshua Hershberger. He's always been *früt* about dogs."

Liz frowned. So he wasn't at the show because of something he'd seen by the river the day before when Purcell was killed.

Amy looked to Liz. "Früt?"

"Crazy."

"Ah."

Liz introduced Miriam and Amy, then asked after Miriam's family.

"Is that the Hershbergers on Oak Lane?" Sadie broke in.

Liz was only familiar with Lowell Hershberger, an elderly man who was friends with her Uncle Amos and built sheds for a living.

"That's right," Miriam said. "He's fortunate to be on his Rumschpringe or he wouldn't be allowed to be wasting time at the Hund show."

Mary Ann rejoined them and handed Miriam a spool of thread. "On the house for causing you so much trouble."

"*Nay*, I must pay," Miriam protested.

"Nonsense." Sadie prodded her toward the door. "It's a gift. Now go on and get back to your sewing. We've kept you long enough."

Miriam made one last vain protest before finally caving to Sadie's pressure and bidding them all *auf wiedersen*.

Amy glanced at her watch as the door closed behind Miriam. "Do you think it'd be a good time to pay Joshua Hershberger a visit?"

Liz tamped down a ripple of nervousness. By how intently Joshua had watched the fallout after the tail-snipping scene at the dog show,

Liz was almost certain he'd seen something, maybe even the person who'd sabotaged Edward's chances of winning. Of course if Rutherford killed Purcell, the tail-snipping was probably connected to his death or John's disappearance. But if Joshua had seen something by the river . . . that was another story. "Okay, but we don't tell the Hershbergers how we found out who Joshua is or where he lives. If they resent our prying, I don't want Miriam facing any backlash because of it."

"Deal."

Mary Ann and Sadie opted to return to their shopkeeping since they didn't want to upset any less-forgiving customers than Miriam. On the drive to the Hershbergers' farm, Amy debated which interrogation method to use on young Joshua. "We could play good cop, bad cop. You, of course, being the good cop."

Liz laughed. "I own the only bed-and-breakfast in town. I'm sure they'll know I'm not a cop. And knowing how reticent the Amish are around the police, the less we say about cops, the better."

"Good point."

Liz parked in front of the Hershbergers' farmhouse, and a woman Liz presumed to be Mrs. Hershberger stepped out on the porch, wringing a tea towel in her hands and eyeing them suspiciously. Liz hopped out of the car and introduced herself and Amy.

The woman visibly relaxed. "Ah, *ja,* I've heard of you. Your *Mutter* was from here."

"That's right. I was wondering if we might talk to your son, Joshua." She stiffened. "Why?"

"One of my guests is missing and we think he might have seen something that could help us locate him."

"Nay. He's said nothing to us." Mrs. Hershberger turned to her door as if that was the end of the conversation.

"Is he here?" Amy piped up.

A young woman stepped out of the barn, carrying a pail of milk to her mother.

"Has Joshua returned?" Mrs. Hershberger asked her.

The young woman surveyed Liz then Amy before answering. "Ja, he's in the *Shetta*."

"In the barn," Liz said to Amy, steering her toward its door.

Mrs. Hershberger hurried past them and disappeared into the barn. The words of their Bernese Swiss dialect soon drifted out the door. Mrs. Hershberger then reappeared and motioned them inside, then hovered behind them as they faced Joshua.

Liz already knew they weren't going to get anywhere with him, so she didn't waste any time beating around the bush. She produced a printout she'd made of John's picture. "Have you seen this man?"

"Nay," he said, betraying no hint of deception.

"Why were you out by the river this morning?"

"I take a shortcut through the field," he said.

"Why did you run when we called to you?" Amy asked.

He glanced past her shoulder, presumably at his mother. "Mutter does not like us to talk to strangers."

"Someone was killed by the river last night, and this man, a guest at my inn, is missing. If you saw anything out of the ordinary that might help us find him, I'd be most grateful if you told me," Liz said.

His gaze slid to his mother once more, and he squirmed. "I can't help you."

Liz stifled a frustrated sigh. He was uncomfortable about something, but it could simply be his mother's scrutiny. "Did you see who clipped the shih tzu's fur at the dog show?"

Surprise momentarily replaced the discomfort in his face. He abruptly turned his attention to the pitchfork in his hand and scooped a load of dirty straw. "Nay. Excuse me. I need to finish my chores."

"Of course. Thank you for your time," Liz said.

Amy shot her a look of irritation, but acquiesced when Liz prodded her toward the door.

When they reached the car, Amy said, "He knew something. It was written all over his face."

"Sure, but he was never going to tell us with his mother standing there. Besides he didn't show any hint of recognizing John, so whatever he's hiding probably wouldn't help us find him."

10

Liz and Amy were finishing up their supper dishes when Chief Houghton appeared at the back door. Liz hurried to let him in. "We were hoping you'd bring us an update. Did Rutherford confess? Does he know where John is?"

The chief looked tired. "Can we sit?"

Liz's hopes dimmed a fraction. Rallying, she offered him a cup of coffee as he took a seat at her kitchen table.

"Rutherford admitted to writing the note," the chief said.

Amy squealed and grinned at Liz. "Are we good at this or what?"

Stan held up a hand to tamp down her enthusiasm. "He did not confess to killing Purcell, and he has a solid alibi for the time of death."

"Oh," Liz and Amy said in unison, slumping in their chairs.

"However, you were partially right about him 'poisoning'"—he made air quotes with his fingers—"Purcell's breakfast yesterday morning. What he claims he did was dump a heavy dose of chocolate laxatives in Purcell's hot chocolate."

"Which was why Purcell assumed he had the flu," Liz finished.

"Exactly." The chief sipped his coffee.

Liz exhaled a frustrated sigh. "So we're no closer to figuring out where John is, let alone proving he didn't murder Purcell."

The chief scrubbed his palm over his whiskered chin, as if debating whether to say something else.

"I guess you don't think whoever snipped the hair from Edward Lock's dog is connected to the attack on Purcell?" Liz asked.

The chief's head tipped curiously at her change in subject. "No."

"Did you know Edward is one of my guests?"

Stan pulled the list of names she'd given him that morning from his pocket. "Yes, I'd already questioned him before the incident at the show."

"And?"

"He claims he was at the inn at the time of the murder. Can you verify that?"

"Well, he joined us for afternoon refreshments, then went upstairs to roll the ball for his dog. I didn't notice him leave, but I don't keep close tabs on my guests."

"You think he might have left?"

Liz frowned. "I don't want to cast undeserved suspicions around, but it occurred to me he's the only guest that didn't have anything nasty to say about Purcell this morning."

"And that makes him look guilty?"

"Well, if he killed Purcell, he wouldn't want to appear as if he had a motive, right?"

"And," Amy said, "if being questioned this morning made him afraid you were on to him, because you must've figured out the corn knife belonged to the inn, he could've snipped his own dog's tail to make himself look like a victim too."

"Presumably a victim of the same fanatic that killed Purcell," Liz added. She shivered at the sudden realization that if she was right, she had a murderer sleeping under her roof. Then she remembered something. "Wait, I don't think it was Edward after all. He wouldn't complain about Purcell's judging because shih tzus are in the toy group, which was Purcell's preferred group to judge. Edward had no motive that we know of."

The chief straightened in his seat, seeming to come to a decision. "And the stab wound didn't kill Purcell."

"What?"

"We can't explain why he was stabbed. Maybe to throw us off the perpetrator's track."

"You mean to make you think the killer was staying at the inn when he wasn't?"

"Possibly. The coroner has now confirmed the knife wound occurred after his heart had all but stopped. Perhaps the perp stabbed him as insurance. Or possibly the stabbing was a calculated act to divert suspicions."

"If his heart had already stopped, that explains why there was so little blood at the scene," Liz said. "But then, what killed him?"

"Tests showed a high concentration in his system of a medication prescribed to heart patients."

"He OD'd on his own medication?" Amy asked.

"No, his heart was perfectly sound," the chief said. "Someone must've spiked his drink with it."

"There was alcohol in his blood too?" Liz asked.

"Yes. It magnified the effect of the drug."

"Could your coroner tell from Purcell's stomach contents what or where he might've eaten?" Amy asked.

Stan slung back the last of his coffee. "You've been watching too many cop shows."

Amy shot Liz an indignant look but refrained from informing the chief that she'd used such evidence more than once in her own cases.

"Can I get you more coffee?" Liz asked.

Chief Houghton shook his head and covered his mug with his hand.

"Were you able to find and question Rhonda Piper?" Liz asked, wanting to glean whatever else the chief knew before he left.

"No, but we have a BOLO out for her. As it turns out, she may indeed have something to do with John's disappearance."

Liz's pulse spiked. "How so?"

"Her fingerprints were all over his room."

Liz gasped. "I can't believe John would've let her in. I guess I need to get better locks on my doors."

"She also has a criminal record. She assaulted her husband. Now ex-husband," Stan added.

"Oh, wow," Amy said.

"Do you think she killed Purcell?" Liz asked.

"I don't know. We haven't found anything to connect her to him."

"Except she was at the dog show, maybe under false pretenses." Just like John seemed to have been. Liz grimaced. She'd forgotten to tell Stan that Peanut apparently didn't belong to John. She preferred to wait until she heard back from "Trish and Bob" as to why John had the dog. Maybe they were friends of his and had given permission for him to take Peanut.

"Yes, but it was John's phone number on Purcell's phone." The chief pushed to his feet. "I need to go. I just figured I owed you an update."

"I appreciate that," Liz said, walking him to the door. "I guess I should be relieved to know my corn knife didn't deliver the fatal blow, but I'll be happier once we know what's happened to John." Liz closed the door behind the chief and turned to Amy. "Are you thinking what I'm thinking?"

She grinned. "You want to hit the bars?"

Liz laughed. "Yeah, there are three restaurants that serve alcohol within a mile or so of where Purcell's body was found. I thought we could start there."

"I'll grab my coat!"

Liz phoned Sadie. "Could you print off a picture of John and one of Rhonda for me from your camera?"

"Sure thing. What are you up to?"

Liz explained their plan.

"Ooh, I wish I could join you, but I have a planning meeting for the living Nativity program at church in an hour. I'll get those printed for you right now, though."

"Great, see you in ten minutes."

Twenty minutes later, photos in hand, Liz and Amy walked into Burke's Family Restaurant. The place was bustling with what looked like a couple of birthday parties and a scout troop meeting.

"Somehow, I don't think this is our place," Amy whispered to Liz.

Liz showed the harassed-looking hostess John's and Rhonda's pictures and asked if she recalled seeing them yesterday.

The hostess shook her head and moved on to the next people in line when she discovered Liz and Amy didn't plan to stay.

"I think at the next place I'll just show John's picture first," Liz said, "because, otherwise, people will think of them as a couple."

"Good idea. It's too bad we don't have a picture of Purcell," Amy added.

"But I do." Liz pulled the dog show program from her purse.

"Perfect." Amy pulled open the door to Murphy's. "I think we might've hit the jackpot."

Scattered among the tables were numerous patrons with dogs curled under the tables at their feet.

"I'm surprised the owner isn't worried about health code violations, letting all those dogs in here."

"Doesn't look as if his patrons are the type to complain."

Liz and Amy approached the bar.

"What can I get you ladies?"

"We're looking for a friend, actually," Liz said. "Have you seen this man in here, by chance?"

"You might want to be choosier about who you befriend."

"Excuse me?"

"Does the police chief know you know this guy?" the bartender needled.

"Yes, as a matter of fact he does," Liz said. *Not that it's any of your business.*

"Well," the bartender said, "like I told the chief, the guy was in here drinking beers with the victim between three and four, yesterday afternoon." He pointed to a table in front of the window. "At that table, right over there."

Liz tamped down a twinge of annoyance that the chief hadn't seen fit to share that tidbit about her missing guest. She understood that he couldn't share everything, but what else was he keeping from her? "Did you have many other patrons at that time?" She motioned to the current ones with dogs. "Any of these?"

"No, people tend to wait until happy hour before meandering in. There was a woman nursing a drink at the bar for a while, though."

Liz pulled out her photo of Rhonda. "This woman?"

The bartender reached across the bar for the photo, his T-shirt sleeves rolled up to offer an optimum view of his bulging biceps. He squinted at the picture. "I didn't get much of a look at her face. She was wearing a knit hat with a visor. But she looked as though she was a regular at the gym."

"Did this woman talk to the two men?" Liz asked.

The bartender filled a waitress's drink order, then turned back to Liz. "No, she glanced at them a few times, though."

Outside, Liz paced the sidewalk. "Well, that didn't help us much. A woman who may or may not have been Rhonda was here at the time of John and Purcell's meeting. But we still have no idea where she is, or any proof that said woman slipped the heart medication into one or both drinks."

"It wouldn't have been difficult. That bartender isn't exactly Mr. Observant. So what now?"

"Let's head back to the inn." Liz wasn't ready to compromise Amy's health by gallivanting about until all hours on a wild goose chase. The moon was almost full and cast an eerie glow on the bare tree branches, stretching to the road like gnarled hands poised to strike.

Dark clouds skittered across the moon and the wind stirred up the fallen leaves along the roadside's edge. Liz rounded a downhill bend just as a deer burst out of the trees.

Slamming on the brakes, she swerved to miss it.

Amy screamed.

Liz overcorrected, throwing the car into a spin. She brought the car to a bone-jarring stop in the center of the road, facing diagonally back in the direction they'd come. "You okay?"

Amy held the dash and the door handle in a death grip. "Just peachy. What was that?"

"Rudolph. Apparently, he lost his way."

"Yeah, that was weird. So you saw the red flash of light too?"

Actually, Liz had been joking about Rudolph, but now that she thought about it, she had seen a flash of red. "It was in the woods."

Liz straightened the car and drove back up around the bend. Spotting a shattered taillight in the center of the road, she said, "I hope that's not mine."

"You didn't hit anything."

Liz pulled a U-turn and parked on the shoulder at the bend in the road, her headlights shining into the trees that had hidden the deer. "You see the red light now?"

Amy lowered her window and squinted into the trees. "Uh, this is kind of a dangerous place to stop the car. It was probably the deer's eyes or something reflecting your headlights."

Liz flipped on her hazards and climbed out of the car. "There are tire tracks trailing off the road." Liz reached through Amy's window. "Hand me the flashlight from the glove box."

Amy handed it to Liz and then climbed out too.

Liz picked her way down the ravine. "Careful, the leaves are slick."

Amy slid a few feet but managed to grab a branch and steady herself. "Yeah, I'm not exactly wearing the best shoes for tromping down a ravine. Please tell me there are no bears or wolves around here."

"There aren't."

"Thank goodness."

Liz swung the flashlight's beam in a wide arc. "It's a car. See it?" She jogged the last twenty feet down the ravine.

Amy lost her footing and tumbled down behind her. She bowled into the back of Liz's legs and sent her over too. "I'm sorry. Are you okay?"

Liz pushed to her feet and brushed rotting vegetation off her hands and knees. "I'm good. What about you?"

Amy rose more gingerly. "I twisted my ankle." She attempted to put weight on it, but cried out and all but fell onto the nearest rock. "I don't think it's bad."

"Wait here," Liz said. She approached the car slowly, all the while sweeping the flashlight's beam over the windows. She couldn't see anyone inside. Her heart raced. She couldn't tell the car's color, except it was light. She swept the beam over the trunk. "It's the same make as John's."

When she reached the driver's door, she aimed her flashlight's beam inside and peered in. "It's him. Call 911."

Amy sprang to her feet, but after one step that made her face twist in pain, she stopped and called from where she stood.

Liz wrenched on the car door, but she couldn't budge it. "I think it's locked or damaged."

"Is he breathing?"

"I can't tell yet." Liz snatched up a rock and smashed the window behind the driver's seat. She reached for the pulse point on his neck.

His pulse was faint, but there. "He's alive! John, can you hear me? It's Liz from the inn."

"The dispatcher needs a location," Amy said.

"At the bend on Jacob's Way, just east of town. Tell them to look for my car." Not getting a response from John, Liz heaved herself part of the way through the back window to reach his door's lock release. "Got you," she murmured, then wriggled back out and yanked open the driver's door.

"John?" Liz panned the beam over his face. He had a cut above his left eye. His dash sat in his lap, his steering wheel pressed to his chest. "They're going to need the Jaws of Life to get him out of here," Liz called to Amy, then took John's hand in hers. "Squeeze my hand if you can hear me."

His hand moved a scant amount and her heart soared.

"Good. Everything's going to be okay. Help is coming."

Liz shone the flashlight at what she could see of his crushed leg and cringed.

"Liz?" he slurred faintly.

Liz clasped his hand once more. "I'm still here. Don't worry. I'm not leaving you. How did this happen? Did you lose control of your car? Did someone hit you?"

"Purce—" His voice faltered.

Her heart jumped to her throat. "He's dead, John," she said quietly, her gaze fixed on him.

His shoulders sagged deeper into the seat and he let out a gut-wrenching groan.

She felt bad and relieved at the same time. Bad that she'd broken the news so abruptly and relieved that the news seemed to upset him. Not the reaction she'd expect from Purcell's murderer.

The sounds of sirens filled the air.

"Help is almost here," Liz soothed.

John's grip tightened, surprising Liz with its strength. "Sss."

"Don't try to talk now," Liz said.

His breathing had grown rapid and shallow, and perspiration beaded his face. "S–son in dan–ger," he wheezed. Then his hand went limp and his head lolled to his shoulder.

11

At the sound of the first emergency vehicle parking, Amy hobbled higher up the ravine, waving the light on her cell phone toward the top. "We're down here. Hurry!" she shouted.

Tears stung Liz's eyes as her fingers desperately searched John's wrist for his pulse. She could still hear the faintest of breathing. Slower now. But there. *Thank you, God.* His pulse was faint and uneven.

The next hour passed in a blur. Paramedics did what they could to support John, as firefighters tore the car off his legs, piece by piece.

Amy refused help from EMS, not wanting to take them away from John. So Officer Jack Gerst, who was first on the scene, helped her up the hill and invited her to sit in his heated cruiser to answer questions.

Officer George Hughes tapped Liz's shoulder, snapping her attention back from the sight of the paramedics slowly bringing John up the hill on the gurney. "He didn't say anything else?"

"No. He was barely able to talk. We need to tell the chief that John said someone's son is in danger."

"Whose son? John's?"

"I don't know. John never mentioned having children." Liz buried her freezing hands in her coat pockets and dipped her nose into the collar. "Someone ran him off the road."

"We don't know that."

"I saw part of his shattered taillight up here. On the road. That must have happened before he hurtled down the ravine."

"Don't worry. We'll figure out what happened."

The paramedics crested the hill with John, and Liz ran to his side. "Is he going to be okay?"

"We've managed to stabilize him," one of the paramedics said, pulling open the ambulance's rear doors. "He's going straight to surgery. The doctors will be able to tell you more after that."

Liz and Amy followed the ambulance to the hospital. Amy didn't want to sit in the ER waiting room to have her ankle examined, so staff on the surgical floor offered her ice to put on it as they sat in the waiting room.

What seemed like hours later, but turned out to be only forty minutes, the door to the room burst open and Liz bolted to her feet. "Is he okay?" Seeing it was the chief, she sagged. "Oh, it's you."

"George filled me in on your discussion with Mr. Baxter. And you were right. It looks as if his car was clipped, sending him off the road. In addition to the broken taillight, there is a black paint scrape across his rear fender."

"Rhonda's car is black."

Stan nodded grimly.

"What about his son? Is he okay?"

"He doesn't have a son."

Liz sank into a chair, confused. "But he said clear as anything 'son in danger.' I know what I heard."

"Purcell has a son," Amy said. "Remember, Purcell's wife died in childbirth three years ago, but his son survived."

"Do you know where Purcell's son is?" Liz asked Stan.

"With his grandmother. They're on their way here from Mississippi."

"Is that where Purcell is from?"

"No, his mother and son were visiting relatives. They should arrive sometime tomorrow afternoon."

Liz shivered, both at the thought of the grief they would have to face when they arrived and for fear of the danger that might await them here. "Anyone could get to them between there and here. Can't you ask the state police to escort them or something?"

"We're on top of this." Stan squeezed Liz's shoulder. "Why don't you go home? Mr. Baxter will be in surgery for hours yet. He's not likely to be conscious before morning."

Liz reluctantly agreed, and she and Amy headed back to the inn.

Liz wrapped Amy's ankle in an elastic bandage to control the swelling and told her to take the bed. She'd planned to give her Rhonda's vacated room, but the stairs would only cause her more pain.

Amy protested.

"It's okay," Liz assured. "I doubt I'll sleep much anyway." Amy, on the other hand, looked ready to drop. Regret chewed Liz's insides that she'd subjected her to all that time out in blustery weather, and then kept her up so late in her already compromised condition.

Liz headed to the kitchen to prep breakfast for the morning, but John's last words haunted her. How were they supposed to keep the boy safe? Was Purcell's son even the one whom John had meant?

If she could figure out why Purcell had called John, she might have a clue who was behind all this.

Beans scratched at the door, asking to go out. Peanut must have heard him, because a second later, he came bounding out of Liz's private quarters, looking eager to join whatever was up.

"Okay, but make it quick." Liz snapped a leash on Peanut since she wasn't sure she could trust him to stay on the property like Beans, and then opened the door without bothering to turn on the outside light. She stepped outside, closing the door behind her.

The bushes near the door rustled. Beans went into a barking frenzy, with Peanut following suit.

"Shh," Liz scolded.

The dogs were oblivious to her.

"Beans, stop it!" The light snapped on in the window of the Heirloom Room above, and Liz gave Peanut's leash a firm tug and lunged for Beans's collar. "Quiet! You're disturbing our guests."

The outside door creaked open, spilling light onto the lawn. Amy poked her head out. "Liz? Is everything okay?"

Beans had stopped barking, but he refused to yield ground.

"Yeah, sorry. The dogs wanted to come out."

Beans growled at the bush, then pounced at its base.

Liz cried out.

"What is it?" Amy called.

The prowler stepped from the bushes and immediately endeared himself to Beans and Peanut by lavishing attention on them. His clothes gave away his Amish heritage a moment before Liz recognized him.

"Joshua? What are you doing here?"

The Amish boy straightened from petting the dogs, pulled his hat from his head, and nervously curled the brim in his hands. "I wasn't completely honest at the *Haus*. My Mutter and *Grossmutter* very much don't want me in trouble with the English."

"Come inside," Liz said. "I'll make some tea."

Amy wrapped her long bathrobe more firmly around her middle and hobbled ahead of them to the kitchen, where she put the kettle on. Liz offered Joshua a seat at the kitchen table. She sat across from him. Beans sprawled at his feet and draped his head adoringly over one boot. Liz didn't know whether to feel reassured that the dog didn't see Joshua as a threat, or worried that he didn't in case it turned out he was. Beans tended to be a good judge of character though, as most dogs were, so she tried to relax.

"You did see something at the dog show," Liz said matter-of-factly. The question she actually wanted to broach was what he'd seen by the river, but she didn't want to scare him off, so she'd take it in baby steps.

"Ja."

"What?"

"I saw who clipped the shih tzu's fur."

Liz nodded. She'd figured as much when she'd questioned him earlier. "Who?"

"The boy with the toy poodle who won the conformation group *Herr* Lock was supposed to compete in."

Liz and Amy exchanged a weighted glance. The culprit didn't sound like someone with any connection to John or a motive to kill a judge who favored toy breeds.

"And why didn't you say anything when it happened?"

"Grossmutter always says not to get involved in the English's business."

Amy filled the teapot and brought it to the table, along with cups and milk, then pulled up a chair.

"And you were near the river the other day?" Liz asked.

His gaze dropped to the table. "Ja."

"What did you see?" she asked gently.

"Nothing. Not really. I was walking along the river back to my Haus after the Hund show, when I heard a thump on the ground behind me. I spun around, thinking it was an animal. It was getting dark and I couldn't see what made the sound right away, so I stood there, waiting for it to move. But it didn't."

"And?" Liz prompted when he paused uncertainly.

"I heard voices at the top of the riverbank. I figured they might've tossed a bottle of beer or something."

"So you looked for it?"

"Ja. I wanted to dispose of it properly. Then I saw the corn knife, smeared with blood."

"You said it was getting dark," Amy interjected. "How could you tell it was blood?"

Joshua squirmed.

"Did you have a flashlight? A cell phone with one?"

Liz hid a smile at the realization Amy was fishing for an admission about John's phone.

Joshua blushed and dug his hand into his coat pocket. But when he pulled it back out, he held a small LED flashlight. "A vendor at the show was handing these out." It was the size of a bike reflector and looked as if it was designed to clip onto a dog's collar.

"Okay," Liz said. "What did you do next?"

"I ran up the hill, but I didn't see anyone."

Liz waited, hoping the silence would induce him to say more. She poured three cups of tea and set one in front of him. "You didn't see the victim?" she finally asked.

Joshua shook his head. "Nay."

Liz sensed he was telling the truth. His voice was steady and he looked a great deal more relaxed now that he'd come clean. "What did you do after that?"

He sipped his tea instead of answering.

"You said this happened as it was getting dark?" Amy said. "But your sister said you didn't get home until after bedtime."

The muscle in his cheek twitched. "I found something else." He reached into his pocket once more, and this time withdrew a cell phone and placed it on the table. "I found this."

"Where did you find it?"

"In the parking lot of the bar with the Hund on the sign. It was ringing."

Instinctively, Liz knew the phone must be John's. Joshua had found it in the right vicinity, about the time Liz had been trying to reach John. She managed to tamp down her urgent need to know if he had seen how John lost it. Maybe he could ID John's attacker, the man who might yet be stalking the son John was so worried about. "Did you see who dropped it?"

"Nay. It was lying on the ground, but there were no cars around."

"Okay, so you heard it ringing." She picked up the phone and turned it on. But that's as far as she got, because it was password protected. "Then what did you do?"

"I couldn't make it work. I walked around and fiddled with it for hours. I could get it to take a picture, but I couldn't get it to do anything else. It kept asking for a password."

"But later the phone rang and you answered it," Liz clarified, certain now he must've been the teenager who'd answered her call. "You were near the Grill House by the Shady Rest Motel."

His eyes widened, looking unnerved by the fact she knew.

"I made the call," she explained. "You don't need to know the password to answer an incoming call."

"I answered. When you asked for someone else, I panicked and lied. Then I turned it off so it wouldn't ring anymore and hid it. I didn't want my *Vater* or Mutter to think I had a phone."

That explained why the cell phone company couldn't ping the phone to get a location on it. But according to the number beside the little bouncing icon on the top of the phone, he'd missed more calls than just Liz's.

"Did anyone else call the phone before you turned it off?" Liz asked.

Joshua hesitated. "Once. Later. When I turned it back on for a few minutes."

"Did you talk to the caller?"

"Ja. He said his name was Bill, and he asked me if I knew where Baxter was. I told him he had the wrong number and shut it off again."

Liz stifled a frustrated sigh. "You're sure you didn't see how the owner lost the phone, or who threw the knife you found?"

"I'm telling the truth."

"Okay." Liz pushed up from the table. "I appreciate your coming to me and being honest. I'll pass the phone and your information along to the police."

His face paled. "You won't give them my name. Please."

Liz had been a patent lawyer, not a criminal lawyer, so she looked to Amy, who'd know better if any of Joshua's testimony might prove useful in prosecuting Purcell's murderer. After all, Joshua didn't see the murder occur, or the victim for that matter. He could only vouch for the time the murder weapon was discarded and the location where John's phone was either lost or made to look that way.

Amy shrugged.

"I'll do my best to keep your name out of it." Liz showed him to the door, and then rejoined Amy at the table.

"Well, at least we have *some* answers. I think it's safe to cross 'the teenager who answered John's phone,' aka Joshua, off your suspect list."

"And the same likely goes for the competitor who clipped Edward's dog's tail. I'd better update the chief." Liz tapped his number on her cell phone, and as it rang, she picked up John's once more to attempt to crack the password.

"Liz, it's late. You should be in bed," the chief said by way of a greeting.

"Are you?"

"No."

"Good." She asked if there was any more news on John. After learning he was still in surgery, she told Stan, without naming names, about Joshua's visit. "Did you want me to bring in the phone first thing in the morning?"

"I can send an officer around for it now if that's okay," he said.

"Sure, I'll wait up." Liz heard the chief talking to someone in the background, asking to have the nearest officer head for the Olde Mansion Inn. When he returned to the call, she asked, "Did you find anything in John's car to indicate his relationship with Purcell—why Purcell would've called him?"

A long sigh sounded over the line, before the chief said, "No."

"Well, if you can crack his password, you might be able to check the contacts and messages on his cell phone."

"Hopefully, he'll just wake up and be able to tell us."

"Right, of course." Liz scrubbed her face, exhaustion suddenly tugging at every muscle in her body.

"Any ideas what Rhonda Piper wanted from John?" the chief asked.

"Rhonda?" Liz gave her head a mental shake to catch up with the topic shift. "None. Why?"

"She drives a black car and her fingerprints were in his room. That makes her a prime suspect in the cause of his accident."

"Right." Liz forced her mind to focus and mentally replayed the exchanges she'd witnessed between the pair. "She'd seemed surprised to see him. And furious. I don't think she followed him to Pleasant Creek. I think it's more a case of she was so furious to see him that she went snooping."

"And maybe didn't like what she found," Stan said as if to himself.

"Like what?" Liz asked.

"Hopefully I'll find that out when I can talk to Mr. Baxter."

The crunch of gravel sounded in the driveway. "I think your officer is here."

"Great. Get some sleep."

"Yeah." Liz clicked off the phone and hurried to open the front door before the officer rang the bell.

By the time Liz handed over the phone, recounted her story to the officer, saw him to the door, and returned to the kitchen, Amy had cleared the teacups from the table and washed them. "Any news on John's prognosis?" The worry in her eyes betrayed the fondness she'd quickly developed for him.

"No news yet."

Amy nodded and they drifted back to the sitting area in Liz's private quarters. "You ever think about Matt?" Amy asked, referring to Liz's self-absorbed ex.

"Not if I can help it." Liz sucked in a deep breath, inhaling the fragrance of the fresh spruce branches they'd cut yesterday morning—was it only yesterday morning? *Hope in adversity. Well, we have plenty of the latter right now.* "Although I do have fond memories of the giant Christmas tree his father used to put in the foyer of his house."

"You were good for Matt."

"Maybe, but he wasn't good for me. I am much more content being single."

"Don't you ever want to get married?"

Liz shrugged.

"Have a serious relationship, at least?"

She didn't usually give it much thought, but Amy's prodding sent her thoughts skidding back to this time last year, when Steve had sent word he wouldn't be able to make it home for Christmas. The prospect of spending Christmas alone had definitely put her in a funk, even though she knew Mary Ann and Sadie would've included her in their celebrations. She smiled at the memory of how Jackson had brightened those dark days before Steve had surprised her by coming home after all. One day Steve would have a family of his own and she would have to share him with his children and in-laws. That might not leave him much time to spend with her. "Yes, I guess from time to time I think about it."

"Christmas can be especially lonely without family. Of course, you have your mother's Amish relatives now."

Whereas Amy had no one. "I meant what I said earlier, Amy. You're welcome to stay here as long as you want."

"I appreciate that, but I was actually thinking about you, not me."

"Me?"

"Yes, you've been here, what? A few years? And you still don't have a special guy in your life."

Liz crossed her arms, not liking where this was going. "Did Sadie put you up to this?"

Amy grinned. "She's not the most subtle person. But I've got to agree with her about one thing."

"What's that?"

"You send mixed signals. If a guy isn't confident you'll be receptive to taking the relationship to a new level, he's going to hesitate."

Liz shook her head. "Jackson and I decided—mutually—to take it slow a few months ago. This isn't Brigadoon. Jackson isn't going to disappear into the mist at midnight."

"No?" Amy had the lawyer-to-criminal look that said, *You're deluding yourself.* "That's what happened to Purcell. And what almost happened to John."

What might soon happen to Amy. Liz's heart twisted. Maybe she did need to reevaluate her life in the relationship department, but now was not the time to worry about the signals she was or wasn't sending Jackson. A man was dead, and they'd almost been too late to save John. She would *not* be too late to protect the son, even if she didn't know who he was.

12

In the kitchen the next morning, a burning smell tickled Liz's nostrils. She abandoned the fruit platter she'd been arranging, yanked open the oven, and groaned. Her mind wasn't on breakfast preparations, as the blackened muffins attested. All she could think about was getting back to the hospital to talk to John, to find out who he thought was still in danger. She snatched up an oven mitt and pulled out the overcooked muffins.

Only three on one end looked too dark. The others seemed salvageable. She put them on a cooling rack and moved on to scrambling eggs.

Beans and Peanut ambled into the kitchen and looked at her—then at the cooling muffins.

Liz rolled her eyes. "This is why you're fat, you know," she said to Beans. "And now you're corrupting Peanut."

Peanut yipped.

"Fine, but just a small piece of the burnt ones." She broke off two pieces and fed them to the dogs. "Now skedaddle so I can finish getting breakfast ready."

She returned to the stove, her mind back on all the questions she had for John. A knock at the utility room door made her jump, sending scrambled eggs to the floor. "Ah! Come in," she called, reaching for the dustpan. "The door's open."

The dogs abandoned their race to the door in favor of cleanup duties.

Jackson let himself in, looked at the burnt muffins and the dogs eating eggs off the floor, and gave her an empathetic expression. "Rough night?"

"Do I look that bad?" Liz said.

He smiled, not bothering to deny it. "Stan filled me in about your finding John Baxter last night."

Her heart jumped. "Did he say how he was? Is he awake? Did he say who else might be in danger?"

Jackson shook his head. "Sounds as if it could be days before he's truly conscious because of the pain medications. His leg was crushed, and he had some internal injuries. But they think he'll be able to walk, once he's healed."

"That's a relief. And what about his warning that a son was in danger? Did Stan figure out who he was talking about?"

"He didn't mention that."

Liz's gut churned. The chief had told her not to worry, that he was on top of it. But what if he wasn't? Yes, she'd found John and more or less proved he wasn't a murderer, but the murderer was still out there. *And he or she had been in my inn.* "Have they picked up Rhonda Piper yet?"

"They still haven't managed to locate her."

Gritting her teeth, Liz returned to her breakfast preparations. Until she knew who John had meant by a son in danger and was sure the police were adequately protecting him, she wouldn't be able to let this go. Liz's mind shifted from the questions she'd had for John to tracking down Rhonda and demanding answers from her.

Jackson helped himself to a cup of coffee. "They did find something else interesting."

"Oh?"

"There were traces in John's blood of the same heart medication that killed Purcell."

"What?" The murderer—Rhonda?—must've poisoned them both at the bar, slipping it into their drinks when the bartender wasn't looking.

"Yeah, they figure Purcell's killer probably had hoped it would be enough to kill John too, but he's a much larger man, so he would've needed a larger dose."

"Is Rhonda their number-one suspect now?"

"Evidence is definitely pointing toward her. I'm sorry their primary suspect is still a guest, or at least a former guest, but I figured you'd want to know."

Amy limped into the kitchen.

"The ankle still sore?" Liz asked.

"Not too bad really." She tossed Jackson a big smile. "Good morning. You're here early." She glanced Liz's way and bounced her eyebrows—code for *this looks promising*. She started humming a tune from *Brigadoon*, cheerfully ignoring Liz's dirty looks. The woman was incorrigible.

Jackson downed the last of his coffee. "Yeah, I should be going. See you later."

"Do tell," Amy said the instant the door closed behind him.

"It's not what you think." Liz filled her in on John's status.

"So we need to find Rhonda."

"Without letting on that we suspect her. Because, if she really did poison John and Purcell, we don't want her turning her sights on us."

Amy's exuberance deflated a tad. "Good point."

"I remember when she checked in she had a drawstring backpack that had a *Burt's Gym* logo on it." Liz transferred her batch of eggs to a heated plate. "We could start there. But first I need to get breakfast served."

Liz and Amy joined Edward and Gloria at the dining table. Tiffany and Tara were breakfasting at Mama's Home Cooking today.

"The radio announcer this morning said William Purcell was poisoned," Edward said between forkfuls of egg. "Makes me think it's a woman. They say poison is their weapon of choice."

"Hmm," Liz said. *Might explain why the perp tried to make it look like a stabbing.*

"Did they say what kind of poison was used?" Gloria asked.

"No."

"If I wanted to do away with someone"—Gloria grew unusually animated waving her empty fork as she spoke—"I'd inject the person with a megadose of insulin. It's undetectable, and if you choose an inconspicuous injection point, chances are the coroner won't even be able to figure out the victim was jabbed with a needle."

Amy cocked her head. "How do you know so much about poisons?"

"I was a nurse for thirty years."

"Ever married?" Liz asked, noticing she didn't wear a wedding band, but her left finger had an indentation at its base that suggested she had been.

"My husband Albert's heart gave out two years ago."

"Oh, I'm so sorry." Liz exchanged a glance with Amy. But she didn't seem to be thinking what Liz was thinking. Of course, knowing about heart medications, and maybe having an old stash of them, hardly made Gloria a viable suspect. She didn't like Purcell's judging biases, but she hadn't appeared to know John at all. Not to mention she drove a silver car, not a black one.

"Burt's Gym is about an hour north of here," Amy said, consulting the map app on her smartphone, as Liz straightened the yoga pants she'd donned to look the part of gym goer. "You okay with being gone for more than a couple of hours? I can drive us."

"Sure, Sarah can take care of things here. I don't have any guests coming in today." Liz stooped to pat Beans and Peanut, who'd become inseparable—the Laurel and Hardy of dogs. "You boys be good while I'm gone."

Mary Ann poked her head around the corner from her shop. "You're going out? You'll be back in time for the costume parade, won't you?"

"I'm not sure there's anything more I can learn at the show," Liz said.

"Still, it'd be a shame to let the entry fee go to waste. Beans looks so adorable in his costume."

"I'll be back in time," Liz said, even though the thought of parading around with Beans in a Santa suit made her cringe. She couldn't disappoint Sadie and Mary Ann, though, after all the work they went to sewing his costume.

An hour later, Amy pulled into the parking lot of Burt's Gym.

Liz climbed out of the passenger seat and looked around. "No sign of her car in the parking lot."

"I hope one of the other members knows where we can find her."

They strolled inside, looked around as if admiring the setup, and headed for the reception desk where a blonde, pony-tailed, twenty-something in skintight workout clothes stood smiling in welcome.

"Hi," Liz said. "I recently met a woman by the name of Rhonda Piper. You know her?"

"Oh, yes, she's one of our regulars."

"I figured. I saw the gym's name on her bag, and she's in such good shape, I thought I should check out the place."

"That's wonderful. I'd be happy to show you around."

"That'd be great. We were going to ask Rhonda if she'd give us a tour, but I haven't been able to get a hold of her the last couple of days. Have you seen her in here?"

Amy grinned at Liz, looking impressed at how smoothly she got to the point of their visit.

"No, I heard she was going to a dog show for the weekend. Research for a college paper, I think."

The gym rep caught the attention of a female member, who

was more Liz's age and body shape, working out on an elliptical machine. "Have you heard from Rhonda the last couple of days?"

"No. She might be staying with her dad again. Ever since he had that heart attack last summer, she's needed to be there a lot."

Liz exchanged a victorious glance with Amy. It sounded as if they might have just proven Rhonda had access to the medication used to kill Purcell and the attempt to kill John.

"Where's Mr. Piper living these days?" Amy asked.

"Oh, no," the woman on the elliptical corrected. "Piper is Rhonda's married name. It was the only good thing she got out of the marriage, so she kept it after he divorced her, rather than go back to Kowalcheleskyov, or something like that."

"Wow, yeah, I can see why."

"Her dad lives in Huntington, a few miles west of here," the woman added obligingly.

"Thanks," Liz said. "We'll have to check in on them."

For appearances' sake, Liz allowed the receptionist to finish the tour, and then thought of another question. "You wouldn't happen to know why Rhonda is so mad at a John Baxter, would you?"

Frowning, the woman seemed to search her memory banks. "I don't think I've ever heard her mention him. Sorry."

"No worries. You've been a great help. If I could just take a pamphlet home with the pricing information, I'll think about it."

At that, the pressure tactics started. The woman offered a free thirty-day trial, and stood poised to collect Liz's phone number and e-mail address for future advertising blitzes, no doubt.

"We'll have to do that next time," Amy interjected, prodding Liz toward the door. "Or we'll be late for another appointment."

Liz waved to the woman and thanked her for her time. Taking Beans to the costume parade wasn't exactly an appointment, but it was close enough if it got them out the door.

By the time they stepped out of the gym, Amy already had directions to a Mr. Kowalcheleskyov, who in all probability, was Rhonda's ill father. A short time later, they pulled into his driveway. Rhonda's black car wasn't there.

In response to their knock, the elderly man tapped on the window and motioned them to let themselves in. "You're early," he said.

"Pardon me?" Liz said.

"With my meal."

"Oh, I'm sorry. We're not the meal-delivery service. We're actually looking for your daughter. Her friend at the gym said we'd probably find her here."

"You with the police?"

"No."

"Because I already told them yesterday she's at a dog show for the weekend."

Liz scanned the small house and couldn't see any evidence Rhonda had been there. She certainly hadn't done any dishes or picked up dirty laundry, if she had been. "Well, thank you for your time, sir." Liz checked her watch. If they left now, they could make it back to Pleasant Creek before lunch. "We'll let ourselves out."

Outside a police cruiser was blocking Amy's car in the driveway and two officers stood beside it, presumably waiting for them. One spoke into the radio at his shoulder and a third officer appeared from behind the house.

"What's going on?" Amy asked.

"We need to ask you a few questions, if you don't mind," one officer said, as the other two seemed primed to thwart an escape attempt.

"What's this about?" Liz asked.

They ignored the question and asked for ID. After scrutinizing their drivers' licenses, the officers seemed to relax a fraction—presumably because Amy and Liz were not who they'd thought—but that didn't stop the one who seemed to be in charge from grilling them about how they knew Mr. Kowalcheleskyov and why they were visiting him.

"We're looking for the same person I imagine you are," Liz said. "Rhonda Piper."

The twitch in the officer's jaw confirmed her suspicion.

"Rhonda stayed at my inn and then skedaddled yesterday morning without settling her bill."

"I just came along for the ride," Amy added.

The third officer looked at each ID in turn and then got on his phone. A minute later, he said, "Let them go."

The other two officers jumped in the cruiser and moved it from behind Amy's rental. The third officer handed back their IDs. "Your police chief asked me to tell you to leave tracking down Rhonda to the professionals."

Liz nodded. What could she say? She was impressed they'd been cooperating with Pleasant Creek police and staking out Rhonda's dad's place.

On the road again, Amy and Liz finally looked at each other and burst into peals of laughter. "I thought I was going to faint back there," Amy admitted. "But I guess I should be flattered that they mistook us for a woman at least ten years younger."

"I guess they figured she was smart enough to know the police would be looking for her car and got a rental instead."

"To think my colleagues thought I'd be bored vacationing in Booniesville, Indiana."

Liz grinned. "I aim to give my guests the full vacation experience." For the rest of the drive back to Pleasant Creek, she regaled Amy with tales of other cases in which she'd managed to get herself entangled.

As Amy reached the outskirts of Pleasant Creek, she said, "So what do we do now?"

Liz's cell phone rang.

"Where are you?" Sadie hissed over the line. "Someone's trying to steal Peanut."

13

Liz rushed into the inn.

In the foyer, a young woman faced off with Sadie. "If you don't produce him this minute, I'll call the police."

"You do that," Sadie shot back.

Liz closed the final few feet in an instant. "Excuse me. May I help you? I'm the inn's owner."

"Someone from this inn called me. I'm assuming because my husband's idiotic business partner brought my dog here then forgot about him when he left." The woman caught a glimpse of Peanut through the window and plowed past Liz, out the door.

The beagle raced up to her, hauling a breathless Mary Ann on the other end of his leash.

The woman dropped to her knees, oblivious to potential grass stains, and scooped the dog into a bear hug. "There you are. Did you miss your mama?" she cooed.

Peanut licked her face with joyous abandon. The woman pushed to her feet and reached for the leash in Mary Ann's hand.

Mary Ann refused to relinquish it. "Who do you think you are? This dog belongs to John Baxter, a guest of this inn."

"No, he was dog-sitting." She looked from Mary Ann to Liz. "My name is Trisha Boyd. You called me. It's my number on Peanut's dog tag. When no one answered the phone this afternoon, I looked up your number to get your address. You can bet the next time I see John Baxter, I'll give him an earful for just leaving my dog."

"He's in the hospital. The police believe someone ran him off the road. That's why he wasn't here for Peanut."

Instead of looking shocked or embarrassed for blaming him, Trisha turned red with fury. "I knew I should've been suspicious of how eager John was to dog-sit for me this weekend. As soon as I drove into town and saw the dog show, I knew he'd involved Peanut in one of his schemes. What was it this time? Some unfaithful husband take him out because he spotted John taking pictures of him?"

"What?" Liz asked. "He's a private investigator?"

"Yes," Trisha snapped.

Liz's mind whirred. So John might've been the sole target all along, and Purcell merely collateral damage because they shared drinks. But then whose son had John been talking about?

Trisha held out her hand. "May I have my dog's leash now?"

"Could I see some ID first?" Liz asked.

The woman rolled her eyes and let out a huff, but she obliged.

A police car rounded the corner.

"No way," Trisha griped. "You called the cops on me?"

"No. That was probably the woman inside. Don't worry, I'll take care of them. But aren't you the least bit concerned about your friend's condition?"

Trisha bit her bottom lip. "I've got enough ulcers worrying about Bob. I swear the two of them make a new enemy every other week."

"Do you know if they have a case involving Rhonda Piper? Or William Purcell?"

"No idea. Bob keeps me out of it as much as possible. No wait, I remember a case they had over a year ago, involving a rich guy named Piper. Why?"

Stan strode up to them. "Piper? Does this have to do with Baxter?"

Liz explained who Trisha was and apologized for the false alarm.

"That's okay. I would've sent Gerst, but thought I should handle this myself." The chief turned his attention back to Trisha. "What can you tell me about Rhonda Piper?"

Trisha was chewing her bottom lip now. "I'm not sure how much I'm allowed to say. Bob probably shouldn't have been talking about John's case with me."

"Whatever you can tell us could be very important," Liz coaxed. "John is still unconscious and—"

Trisha gasped. "I didn't realize the accident was that serious."

"Yes, and in a brief moment of clarity, he said someone else was in danger. A little boy, we believe. But we don't know who. And unless we figure that out, we won't be able to keep the boy safe."

Stan scowled, probably not appreciating Liz's liberal use of *we* after he'd repeatedly told her to stay out of it.

Trisha sighed and gave in. "Ralph Piper is a wealthy businessman who hired John to spy on his then-wife. I'm not sure if Rhonda was her name or not. He had a prenup that excluded his wife from any settlement if she was unfaithful, which he suspected she was. John proved it, probably with pictures."

Liz looked to Amy. "Revenge is a pretty strong motive for her to go after John."

"But why the boy?" the chief mused.

Trisha shook her head. "I don't know anything about a boy. Or about that other name you mentioned. Like I said, Bob usually tries to keep me out of it." She withdrew a business card from her purse and wrote a number on the back. "That's Bob's cell phone number. You could call and ask him. He and John each work their own cases, but they sometimes talk about them with each other." Trisha snagged the leash out of Mary Ann's loosened grip. "May I go now?"

Liz looked to Stan, in case he had any more questions.

"Yes, thank you for your help," he said. As she headed to her car, Stan turned to Liz and Amy. "The police are on the lookout for Miss Piper. Trust us to do our jobs." He strode off, sparing Liz from having to agree.

Mary Ann glanced at her watch. "Look at the time! We'd better hurry in and get Beans ready for the costume parade." She bustled toward the front door.

Amy was already thumbing numbers into her phone as they followed Mary Ann inside. From the sounds of it, Bob answered. Amy explained the situation and asked what he knew about the case that brought John to Pleasant Creek. When he claimed he didn't know, Amy pressed, dropping Purcell's name and sharing their fear his son might be in danger from someone connected to the case.

He said something Liz couldn't make out.

Amy advised him that the chief would also be calling, asked him not to mention her call, then disconnected. "All he could tell me was that John was working on a missing person's case and the client didn't want him talking about it to anyone else, including his partner."

"So the question is, was Purcell his client? Or the person he was trying to track down for his client? Or neither?"

"And how is Rhonda connected?" Amy added.

Mary Ann and Sadie appeared on the front porch, tugging a reluctant Beans. He wore a red Santa suit, complete with hat and potbelly, and he wore a pair of saddlebags. The one on the right said *Nice* and had small stuffed dolls poking out the top. The one on the left said *Naughty* and bulged with lumps of coal made from black felt. Sadie beamed. "What do you think?"

"It's adorable!" Amy stooped in front of Beans and whispered, "Those girl dogs won't be able to take their eyes off of you."

Beans seemed to perk up at that as if he'd actually understood.

Liz glanced at her watch, feeling torn. She didn't want to disappoint Sadie and Mary Ann after all the work they'd put into the costume, but she didn't want to miss Purcell's mother when she arrived to identify his body, and she really hoped John awoke before that to find out what he'd meant by *son in danger*. "Are you two coming to watch the parade?" Liz asked.

"Wouldn't miss it," Mary Ann said.

"Already closed up the shop," Sadie added. "Do you want to come in my van?"

"No, I think we'd better drive separately. I want to pop by the hospital on the way to look in on John." Liz looked to Amy. "Would you mind waiting with Beans in the car for a few minutes while I run up to his room?"

"No need," Mary Ann said. "We can take him with us and meet you ringside. Just don't be late."

Liz's chest twinged. "I won't."

Fifteen minutes later, Liz and Amy strolled into John's room and stopped short at the sight of a young woman going through his coat pocket and an elderly gentleman searching the drawer beside his bed.

"Who are you? What are you doing?" Liz asked.

The man straightened and smiled warmly. "Just visiting. We're friends of the family."

"What are you looking for?" Amy asked.

Liz glanced at John, hoping they hadn't done anything to harm him.

"We're looking for something that might tell us why he was in Pleasant Creek," the man said. "We only found out about his accident from a news report. He's not from here, you know."

"I know. He was staying at my inn," Liz said. "And who did you say you were?"

"I'm sorry." The gentleman extended his hand. "I'm Henry James and this is my daughter, Victoria. John's father and I go way back. Golfing buddies."

"I see," Liz said, not at all convinced. She was pretty sure she'd overheard John tell one of the other guests his parents had passed away years ago. Of course, John could've been lying about that too. She imagined PIs said whatever they needed to elicit information. "Have you spoken to the police? I'm sure they'd like to talk to you."

"Yes, I'd planned to go there next. Did John mention to you why he was in town?"

Victoria tugged on her father's arm and whispered something in his ear.

Henry brushed her off and looked at Liz expectantly, a forced smile on his face.

"He was here for the dog show. He entered his dog in a few events."

"Ah, yes, that makes sense."

Liz's eyes narrowed. Since John didn't own a dog, which Henry James would know if he was a friend, her suspicions of him mounted. "I'm headed to the dog show now, if you'd like me to show you the way."

"Thank you for the offer, but no. Like I said, we want to pay the police station a visit."

For a long minute they all stood frozen in a silent standoff, each waiting for the other to be the first to leave. Finally Henry James and his daughter murmured goodbye to the sleeping John and slipped out.

Liz waited until they rounded the corner at the end of the hall, then motioned Amy to join her in pursuit. Liz snuck around the corner in time to see them get on a descending elevator. "Stairs," she said.

Liz raced down the stairs just as Henry and Victoria headed out the front door. She hurried to the glass doors and watched as they climbed into a midnight-blue BMW. Because of her tender ankle, Amy trailed behind Liz, but soon caught up.

"Come on!" Liz said.

They hurried as fast as Amy could go to Liz's car and then trailed the BMW as far as the police station.

"I guess he was telling the truth about that much," Amy said.

Liz parked curbside a block away. "Let's wait and see." Her phone rang.

"Liz, where are you?" Mary Ann asked. "We've already checked Beans in. The parade starts in eleven minutes."

"Almost there," Liz said, as Henry James and his daughter entered the police station. Liz started her car. "Don't worry. I'll make it."

Liz sped the few miles from the hospital to the fairgrounds and left Amy in the parking lot with the keys to find a spot to park. An announcement that the parade was about to begin boomed out of the PA system as she rushed inside. She spotted Mary Ann lined up with Beans in the middle of a long row of costumed dogs and slowed. After all, Mary Ann and Sadie had done all the work on the costume, it was only right one of them should get the chance to show it off.

But Mary Ann spotted her and vigorously waved her over. Sadie caught sight of the activity and intercepted Liz with the entry number she needed to pin on.

Liz quickly did so and took Mary Ann's place in line.

The parade of costumed dogs wound its way around the perimeter of the entire building. Beans, lazy as he was at the best of times, dragged his feet, until they approached the border collie he'd mooned over in his last competition, watching from the sidelines with her owner. Then he practically strutted, and Liz was sure he was sucking in his considerable paunch.

As they returned to center stage for one more turnabout, Mary Ann, Sadie, and Amy cheered wildly. Beans almost seemed to grin.

"You like all this attention, don't you?" Liz teased.

Dogs of every shape and size, wearing everything from tutus—à la the ballerinas of *The Nutcracker*—to elf costumes, to superhero suits, lined up in front of the panel of judges. The judges walked down the line, surveying the dogs and their costumes, and scratching scores on their clipboards. Then they retired to the corner to compare notes.

Liz scanned the crowd, looking for Rhonda. Not that she'd expected to find Rhonda back here, even if it was where she'd told her father she'd be. Liz's temper flared at the thought of the woman.

"That's you," the woman beside Liz tapped her arm.

"Pardon me?"

"Your dog won! They're calling you up."

"He did?" Liz looked at the judges, who waved her forward, then to Sadie who was jumping up and down, clapping and shouting like a game-show winner. "Wow, Beans. I guess you just have that *je ne sais quoi* that everyone finds irresistible." Liz led him to center stage and accepted the ribbon.

Beans plopped down beside her and raised a paw as if waving to his loyal subjects. Everyone laughed and waved back.

Sadie raised her camera and snapped a picture.

Liz walked Beans to her friends and gave them each a big hug, then handed Mary Ann the ribbon. "I think you should hang this in Sew Welcome, since the prize really goes to you two for the adorable costume."

Mary Ann began to protest, but Sadie rode right over her with, "Oh, and we can hang the picture of Beans in the costume beside it!"

Amy hunkered down and fussed over Beans. "Don't listen to them. It was your personality that won over those judges, you sly dog." Straightening, she grinned at Liz. "While you were on parade, I heard that the fur-snipping culprit Joshua identified was stripped of his award."

"He confessed?"

"His mother forced him to come clean after she found the hunk of dog fur he'd snipped in his pocket. He should have dropped it on the ground. I told you criminals tend not to be very smart."

Liz laughed.

Gloria bustled through the crowd toward them. "Liz, were you still looking for that obnoxious woman who left the inn early?"

"Yes, have you seen her?"

"Loitering in the parking lot just now. West end. If you hurry, you might be able to catch her."

Liz bolted for the door, refusing to think about the consequences if she didn't catch Rhonda.

14

"Call the chief," Liz called to Amy over her shoulder. She raced for the west door of the fairgrounds with Beans in tow, his little saddle-bags flopping against his ribs.

She hit the exit bar at a dead run and was momentarily blinded by the burst of sunshine after being inside.

Beans barked and took off, yanking Liz with him. Part of her was surprised by how fast he could actually move those short legs.

Liz spotted Rhonda in the parking lot, just like Gloria had said. A man in a dark-blue overcoat handed her a fat envelope, and she handed him a small computer tablet. Liz raced toward them with Beans still in the lead, only to have him suddenly veer the wrong way.

"Stop!" Liz shouted.

Rhonda fled. To Liz's horror, the man lunged at her. Liz shrieked. Growling, Beans hurled himself at the man and sank his teeth into the man's left leg.

Liz's would-be attacker seemed to change his mind and turned to flee.

She caught hold of the man's flapping coat, but couldn't hang on. The man jumped into a black car and sped off.

She looked down at Beans who met her gaze, wagging his stubby tail. "Good boy," she told him fondly.

"Over there," a voice shouted. Amy was coming their way as fast as she could and pointing to Rhonda, who zigzagged through the parking lot.

Rhonda punched her key fob, apparently having forgotten where she'd parked. Amy made a beeline for the car that beeped in response, while Liz circled around to cut off Rhonda's escape path.

Cruisers wailed up the street, lights flashing, and blocked the parking lot exits.

Rhonda turned on her heel and raced toward the crowds pouring out of the building to see what all the excitement was about. Her gym membership was paying off. The woman was fast.

Liz chased after her, but fell farther and farther behind.

Thankfully, the cops had already anticipated the maneuver and outflanked her. Officer Gerst nabbed her three feet from the door.

Liz and Amy caught up to them, panting, as he escorted her out in handcuffs.

"Good work," Stan said, also joining them. To the crowd he said, "Go back inside, folks. Show's over."

Whispering arose, but within a few minutes, most people dispersed.

"An older guy in an overcoat gave Rhonda an envelope in exchange for a tablet," Liz said to the chief. "I almost had him too." She rubbed her fingers together. They'd come away gummy after catching hold of his coat. She sniffed her fingers. The residue smelled like pine.

"Fine," Rhonda blurted. "I stole John's tablet from his room. I'd only planned to borrow it. I just wanted to see what case he was working on so I could ruin it for him like he ruined me. But it took me a long time to crack his password and find the files, and when I snuck back to his room to return it, a light flashed across the room and I rushed back to my room with it."

Liz nodded. That explained the light she thought she'd seen that night.

"The next morning when the police searched his room," Rhonda went on, "I panicked. I thought he'd reported the tablet stolen."

The chief stood there and listened and waited for her to say more.

Liz could tell he was itching to ask a question, as was she. But he had yet to read her her rights and was probably worried she'd clam up once he did. On the other hand, anything she freely babbled was fair game for the cops to use against her.

Rhonda went on. "When I heard John was missing—"

"*Heard*?" Liz interjected. "The police have proof a black vehicle ran him off the road. You drive one of those."

Chief Houghton shot her a glare.

Rhonda's face paled. "It wasn't me!" She looked from Liz to Amy to Chief Houghton. "You have to believe me."

"I went to her car when she beeped it," Amy piped up. "All the light covers are intact and none look as if they are recent replacements. I didn't see any scrapes in the paint either."

"The other guy took off in a black car," Liz added.

Stan nodded and Rhonda latched on to the out.

"Yeah, I had no idea what happened to John," Rhonda said. "I just saw an opportunity to use what he'd found to get back some of the money he'd cost me."

"Because of the divorce?" Amy clarified.

"Exactly." Her indignation with John over how he'd ruined her life returned full bore. "At first his client balked at paying me instead of John for the information. I said 'no problem' and hinted that I was sure a few media outlets would be happy to pay for it. Of course it wasn't long before he called back and told me to meet him here at three. Said he'd pay what I wanted."

"It's only 1:30," Liz said, puzzled.

Stan's jaw tightened. "Henry James and his daughter were in my office when Amy called. They claimed the exchange was set for three p.m."

"Henry James was John's client?" Liz asked.

"That's what he claimed."

"He's lying about the time," Rhonda insisted. "One of his employees called this morning and changed it." She tried to reach into her pocket, but was thwarted by her handcuffs. "See for yourself. The number will be on my phone. I've only had that call and one from my dad today."

Officer Gerst retrieved the phone from her pocket and handed it to the chief. Liz glanced at the call-history screen over his shoulder. The one call was identified as *Dad*. The other was local.

"That's the number for the Shady Rest Motel," Liz said. "I remember it from their sign out front. It was distinctive: 1-2-3-4."

"And Mary Ann spotted what looked like the plastic from a broken car light in their parking lot," Amy chimed in. "A light that could've been damaged while ramming John's car."

"Why'd Henry James come to you?" Liz asked the chief.

"He wanted us to oversee the exchange and arrest his blackmailer." Stan motioned Officer Gerst to put Rhonda in the cruiser. "We'll finish this discussion at the station."

"Did Henry James tell you he went to the hospital to see John?" Liz asked, trailing Stan to his car. "Because he told me he was a friend of John's dad. Which I knew was a lie."

"He hired Mr. Baxter to find his illegitimate son. I understand why he wouldn't want to reveal that to a nosy stranger."

Liz frowned. It stung a little to be called nosy by this man she respected so much.

"I appreciate your quick action," he added.

Liz couldn't tell whether he was trying to soften the blow of calling her nosy or end the conversation. Maybe both. "Did Henry say why he wanted to find his son?"

"He claims his father paid off his college sweetheart and coerced him into a more 'suitable' marriage. But now he says he wants to do right by his son."

"Yeah, likely story," Rhonda mocked as Officer Gerst prodded her into the back of his cruiser. "If he wasn't worried about the dirty secret coming out, why pay me off?"

"Did John find Henry's son?" Liz asked Stan. "Is that the son John meant was in danger?"

"We don't know. If Mr. Baxter had already located him, he had yet to inform James. At least that's what he says."

Liz shook her head. One would think a professional investigator would be too astute to take on a case in which the client might turn around and bump off the person the PI was hired to find.

"Henry says he tried contacting Mr. Baxter after the blackmail call, but couldn't get an answer," Stan said. "Unfortunately, we haven't managed to crack the password on Mr. Baxter's phone to verify the claim."

"So failing to get hold of his PI is what made Henry call Rhonda back?"

Stan hesitated. "He claims his daughter came up with the idea of pretending to go along with the blackmail payoff so they could see if the blackmailer had legitimate information and have her arrested at the same time. It wasn't until Henry was nearly to Pleasant Creek that he heard on the radio about Mr. Baxter's condition."

"You believe him?"

"I don't know. The guy you saw make the payoff could've been an associate who will presumably tell Henry what he wants to know."

Liz's heart thumped. "Or it could've been Purcell's murderer tying up loose ends."

Sadie and Mary Ann insisted that Liz, Amy, and Beans join them for cupcakes at Sweet Everything to celebrate Beans's big win. Liz agreed and led the way back to the inn with Amy and Beans riding with her. She hated not being able to listen in on Rhonda's interrogation, but between what Rhonda could tell the police and what they could get out of Henry, the chief should be able to sort out who Henry's son was and if he was who John had been so worried about. He couldn't have meant Purcell, since she'd already told John that Purcell was dead.

Her stomach twisted. John could still have meant Purcell's son—the theory she'd been operating on since yesterday. If Purcell was Henry's illegitimate son and he or someone else wanted him dead, the motive had to be to avoid future scandal or future claims to the estate. Either way, it stood to reason the killer would want Purcell's offspring dead too.

Then again, maybe Purcell wasn't Henry's son. Maybe John hadn't even been in town for Henry's case. Maybe Purcell was another client, with his own enemies. After all, if Purcell was someone John had been hired to spy on, they wouldn't have shared a drink in the bar. Right?

As Liz drove past the police station, she glimpsed Officer Hughes escorting a woman in her late fifties and a young boy inside. Purcell's mother and his son? Liz pulled into a curbside parking space.

Sadie, driving with Mary Ann, honked from her van as she passed, probably assuming Liz had pulled over for a doggy pit stop.

"I'd like to wait here for Purcell's mother," Liz explained to Amy. "Do you mind driving ahead and letting Mary Ann and Sadie know I'll be a few minutes? I can walk the rest of the way."

"Sure. Do you want me to take Beans so you can go inside?"

Liz mentally debated the idea as she let him out of the back of the car. "No. It's probably better if I look like I just happen to be out here walking the dog." She searched for the fasteners to relieve him of his costume. "I can't figure out how they got this thing on him."

Amy laughed. "Leave it on. He seems to like it."

Beans panted, his tongue lolling, looking oddly pleased with himself.

"All right, but don't say I didn't try," she teased him.

Fifteen minutes later, the woman and young boy reemerged, accompanied by a police officer, and Liz hurried in their direction, with Beans uncharacteristically trotting beside her. The woman's eyes were red-rimmed, and she had a wad of tissue clasped in her hands. The boy, who presumably had been spared hearing any of the details, seemed oblivious to what it all meant. He grinned from ear to ear at the sight of Beans.

"Look, Grandma!" he squealed. "Can I pet him?"

"Of course you can," Liz said as the woman looked questioningly at Officer Hughes.

"This is Liz. You can trust her," the officer said.

Liz offered the woman a smile, then said to the boy, "His name is Beans, and he loves being fussed over."

"Hi Beans, I'm Timmy." The boy dropped to his knees in front of Beans, who rewarded him with sloppy kisses. Timmy laughed.

The woman shot Liz a grateful smile through her tears.

The radio on Officer Hughes's shoulder beeped, and dispatch called a code Liz wasn't familiar with. Hughes touched the woman's elbow. "Mrs. Purcell, are you okay to get back on your own?"

She nodded, and he quietly answered the call as he jogged toward his cruiser.

Liz hadn't expected such a perfect opportunity to speak to Mrs. Purcell. Did this mean the chief had identified the killer? That he was confident Purcell's son wasn't the son John feared was in danger?

Liz expressed her condolences to Mrs. Purcell and invited her to share a cup of tea and a cupcake.

Timmy hugged Beans, as his grandmother looked ready to decline. "Can he come too?"

"Absolutely. He loves cupcakes."

Timmy switched his attention to his grandmother. "Can we, Grandma? Pleeease."

The woman relented with a tired-sounding sigh. "Okay. But just one cupcake."

Liz motioned up the street to Naomi's bakery and the inn, and fell into step beside the pair.

"Did you know my son?" Mrs. Purcell asked. "From the dog shows?"

A natural assumption, considering Beans's getup, and one Liz was tempted to let stand in the hopes it'd encourage her to be more forthcoming, but Liz couldn't bring herself to lie to this grieving mother. "No, but I've heard about him from some acquaintances of his who are guests at my inn. I know at least one man who held your son in high esteem."

"William knew so many people." She let out a sigh. "Ruffled a lot of feathers too. Judging." She gulped. "But I can't believe someone would go this far."

Liz's stomach fluttered nervously. Mrs. Purcell wasn't talking as if the police had identified his killer, and if not, how could they be sure her grandson wasn't in danger?

"You think one of the dog show competitors poisoned him?" Liz asked quietly.

Mrs. Purcell shrugged. "Who else? Every year at least one or two lash out at him over their scores."

"Were you able to give the police names?"

"No. I don't know any names. He didn't talk about it much. Although at one show I went to, there was a woman with a chow chow who gave him a tongue lashing in the parking lot right in front of Timmy and me."

Liz's heart thumped. *Gloria Hunt?*

Sadie must've spotted them coming up the street, because she burst out the door of the bakery, calling, "Here they are!"

"What's going on?" Mrs. Purcell asked anxiously.

"Beans won the costume parade and that woman made his costume. She's probably eager for everyone who wasn't there to see it."

"Oh, then we shouldn't intrude."

"No, no, it's fine." Liz hadn't yet broached the subject of Timmy's welfare. There was no way she could let her go yet. "Besides you look like you could use a cup of tea."

Mrs. Purcell wilted. "Yes, I could."

Sadie held the door open for them as they paraded Beans inside to a round of applause.

Naomi presented him with a special, dog-cookie-topped cupcake and Beans let out a grateful *woof.*

Everyone laughed, even Mrs. Purcell, making Liz glad she'd suggested coming here.

Liz ordered two teas and a hot chocolate for Timmy. Sliding into a booth, she introduced the Purcells to Sadie, Mary Ann, Naomi, and Amy.

"Call me Emma," Mrs. Purcell said.

Sadie and Mary Ann gave her a warm welcome, then immediately volunteered to help Timmy pick a cupcake and to order for everyone.

Emma dabbed at her eyes. "You don't even know me and you're all being so nice."

Liz gave her a sideways hug. "You looked as if you could use a friend. I know I sure appreciated people's small kindnesses when I lost my mom."

Emma nodded. "It's just so hard to believe. And I don't know how to tell Timmy. He's so young, and his dad has always traveled a lot. I don't think it'll really sink in for him for some time."

Amy sat across from Emma and leaned over the table to ask in a low voice, "Did the police express any concern that Timmy might also be in danger?"

The woman's breath hitched. "Why would you think that?"

Liz cringed. She supposed there was no delicate way to broach the subject she'd been dancing around the entire way to the bakery, but she hadn't expected Amy to just plunge in like that. "I had a guest who was also poisoned," Liz explained and relayed John's cryptic warning.

Mrs. Purcell's eyes darted nervously between the women as she wrung her hands.

Naomi delivered their tea and hot chocolate to the table and immediately withdrew.

"The police asked me if William ever received threats against the family," Emma admitted, her voice quavering. "But he hasn't, at least not that he ever told me. Who would do that? You think this man—your guest—was talking about my grandson?"

"I don't know. The last I talked to the police, they hadn't figured out who John had been referring to, so I was a little surprised the officer who'd been escorting you would just leave."

Emma gazed at her grandson. "There's no reason anyone would want to hurt Timmy," she said, only uncertainty rippled her words.

"Can you think of any reason your son might've wanted to talk to a private investigator?" Liz asked gently.

Emma turned white. "Why would you ask that?"

"My guest, John Baxter, the man who met with your son shortly before he died, is a private investigator."

Timmy returned to the table, excitedly displaying his bright-green cupcake.

Emma abruptly stood. "We need to go."

"But Grandma, I haven't had my cocoa yet," Timmy protested.

Emma scooped up her coat and turned to Liz, who would have to move to let her out of the booth. "We need to go," she repeated.

15

Liz rose slowly, not wanting to let Emma leave. "I'm sorry if I've upset you," Liz said gently. "That wasn't my intention. Please, have your tea before you go."

Sadie, holding a plate of cupcakes, and Mary Ann stood behind Timmy, who looked pleadingly at his grandma.

Emma relented and laid her coat back down.

Sadie set the plate on the table, and then she and Mary Ann made their excuses. The new Christmas bell above the door jangled as they exited the bakery.

"I didn't mean to make your friends uncomfortable," Emma said. "I shouldn't be here."

"You didn't," Amy reassured. "They already had their tea. And they were talking about needing to get back to their quilt shop before the two of you even got here."

Liz told Emma about Sew Welcome, and the women who gathered there to make quilts.

"You're very fortunate to have so many friends," Emma said.

Liz glanced at Amy. "Yes, I seem to be reminded of that a lot lately." Liz edged a cup of tea in front of Emma and then held out the plate of cupcakes.

"Thank you," Emma said softly, accepting one.

"You know, I have an empty room at my inn." Liz knew Amy wouldn't mind giving up the room she'd yet to move into. "You and your grandson are welcome to use it at no charge. It'd probably be good for you to stay nearby until the police—" Liz cut off what she'd been about to say, uncertain how much Emma's grandson would understand.

Emma was shaking her head anyway.

Liz recalled what she'd said about a woman with a chow chow bawling out William and had second thoughts about whether she'd be any safer in the inn than her own home.

Timmy downed his hot chocolate and beamed at them, remnants of the drink and his green-frosted cupcake all around his mouth. "That was good."

"What do you say?" Emma prompted.

"Thank you," he said to Liz.

Emma pushed aside her half-empty cup of tea. "Now we really need to go. But let's march you back to the restroom first and get that icing cleaned off you."

Timmy licked frosting off one finger and then extended his hands to Beans to finish the job.

Amy cringed and Liz had to muffle a giggle as Beans happily complied.

The bell jingled, and Liz gasped at the sight of Henry James and his daughter ambling into the shop.

Emma tracked Liz's gaze and immediately snapped her attention back to the table, her face ashen.

Liz pretended not to notice Henry and his daughter as Emma shielded her face with her hand and sank into her seat. "How do you know Henry?" Liz asked scarcely above a whisper.

"Did he see me?" Emma hissed.

"I don't think so," Amy, who sat with Timmy on the opposite side of the table, facing the door, reassured.

"Grandma, who you hiding from?" Timmy asked loudly.

Henry, who'd gone straight to the counter, turned toward the sound of Timmy's voice at the same time Emma snuck a peek in his direction, like a person passing a train wreck, unable to keep from looking.

She snapped her attention to the wall.

However they knew each other, it clearly wasn't amiable. Liz nodded at Henry and fluttered her fingers in a friendly wave, hoping to draw his attention from Emma who was clearly terrified at the prospect of being recognized.

Henry's gaze, however, remained fixed on Emma's profile, and Liz's curiosity about how Emma knew him escalated by the second.

"Dad?" Henry's daughter asked. "What is it?"

Henry didn't answer her.

Amy wrapped a protective arm around Timmy and shrank as far as she could into the corner of the booth. "He's coming this way."

Henry approached the booth in halting steps, looking simultaneously like a man with a new lease on life and a man walking to the gallows.

"What do you want us to do?" Liz whispered to Emma, without taking her gaze off Henry as she continued to try to shield Emma from view.

"Intercept him. I'll sneak out the back with Timmy. Is there a back door?"

"Yes, Naomi can show you." Liz sprang to her feet and blocked Henry's path, giving Emma the space to get out of the booth behind her. Liz could hear Timmy scuffle out as well, asking his grandma who the man was.

"Mr. James," Liz said brightly. "Were the police able to help you?"

Henry didn't even seem to see Liz. He sidestepped her and called after the departing figures. "Emma? Is that you? It's Henry. Henry James."

Liz attempted to once again block his line of sight, but he was having none of it.

A moment before Emma would've slipped out of sight around the corner of the back hall, she wavered. She paused and seemed to be coming to a decision. Then she sent Timmy off to a back room with Naomi and turned to face Henry. "How could you, Henry?" She stalked toward him with surprisingly self-assured steps. "I kept my side of the bargain. I told William his father was dead. I don't know what possessed him to hire a private investigator."

"What?" Henry looked momentarily confused. "No. *I* hired Baxter."

Liz's heart spiked. Henry James was William Purcell's father?

Emma planted her feet in front of Henry and glowered up at him. "Why? To make sure William never found you? Would it have been so bad for him to learn the truth?"

Henry grabbed her upper arms and shook her. "No, listen to me. I want to know our son."

Beans shot out from under the table and growled at him. For a moment, it was as if the Santa costume didn't exist. The bulldog was sending a clear message.

Henry got it and dropped his hold.

The boldness that had seized Emma vanished. Her posture sagged. Her limbs trembled. "Want to . . . ?" she repeated, disbelievingly. Tears pooled in her eyes. Then she abruptly shook her head. "He's dead. *Dead.*" She clenched her fists and drew a deep breath, as if summoning a fresh bout of courage. "You expect me to believe you or your father didn't have something to do with that?"

The room fell silent.

Henry gaped at Emma. "Dead?" he finally said in a hoarse, disbelieving whisper.

Victoria's arm shot around his waist a second before his legs gave way. "It's okay, Dad. I'm here. Sit down." She helped him to a chair.

Emma stared at him warily, as if she wasn't sure she believed he hadn't known.

Liz exchanged a confused glance with Amy, struggling to make sense of what was going on.

"The man who was poisoned?" Henry managed to force out as

if squeezing air through a pinhole. His hand went to his chest, curled in a fist against it.

Victoria retrieved a bottle from his pocket. "Dad, you need to calm down." She spilled out a pill and told him to put it under his tongue.

He swatted her hand away, his gaze still fixed on Emma. "William Purcell? He was my son?"

His daughter pulled out her cell phone, clearly worried about her father's health.

Emma straightened her shoulders and squared her chin. "Yes. I married Arthur Purcell when William was two years old, and he adopted William. He was a good man and a good father."

Tears dribbled down Henry's craggy face. "I wanted to be there for him. For both of you. You have to know that. A part of me died the day you left."

"You mean the day your father sent me away?" Emma grasped the edge of the counter, the color draining from her fingers. "I didn't see you trying to stop him."

Liz glanced at Henry's daughter to try to gauge how critical Henry's agitated state might be to his health, but Victoria kept her eyes on her cell phone.

"He threatened to destroy your family," Henry said to Emma. "To disown me. To make it impossible for me to make any kind of life for us."

Emma let out a disgusted huff. "Lots of people live just fine without their daddy and his giant corporation paying the bills for them."

Henry closed his eyes and lowered his head, looking gutted and ashamed.

A scuffle rose from the direction of Naomi's office, followed by Timmy's high-pitched voice. "I want to see my grandma!"

Henry's gaze snapped to Emma who'd already begun to back toward the rear of the store. "You're a grandmother?"

Panic filled Emma's eyes.

"Is the child William's?" Henry asked breathlessly.

Emma pressed a hand to her mouth and sped up.

Henry stood. "Is he my grandson?" he demanded.

Victoria caught him by the shoulder. "Dad, you're frightening her."

"Keep them here," Liz whispered to Amy and hurried after Emma.

In Naomi's office, Emma comforted her sniffling grandson.

"I'm sorry," Naomi whispered to Liz over their heads. "He heard his grandmother yelling and got scared. I couldn't calm him."

Liz closed the office door. "I think we need to sneak them out of here. Henry looked devastated by the news, but I'm not sure we can trust him."

Emma held her grandson close and looked beseechingly at Liz. "If I go home, he'll find me."

"Don't worry," Liz said. "We'll find somewhere safe for you. Somewhere he'd never think to look."

An Amish horse and buggy clopped up the street outside Naomi's office window.

"Give me a couple of minutes."

Liz hurried out the back door and flagged down the buggy. "Oh, Miriam, I'm so glad it's you. I need your help." Liz quickly explained Emma's need for a place to hide.

Miriam didn't hesitate. "They will stay with me until they are safe."

"We have another problem," Liz said. "Henry is in the shop. We can't let him see Emma and her son get in a buggy or he'll know exactly where to start looking."

"We can bundle them in our coats and *Kapp*."

"Perfect. Then we can sneak them out the back door and into the buggy."

"Ja, no one will notice them."

Liz nodded. They still needed a diversion to make it look as if Emma and Timmy had driven off on their own. It was time to call the chief.

Miriam turned around in the buggy and spoke to two of her children in the back seat. A moment later she handed Liz their coats and a *Kapp*. "We'll wait here. Send them out when you're ready."

Liz raced inside with the clothes. She ducked into the back room while Henry and his daughter continued what looked like an intense argument. "Where's your car parked?" Liz asked Emma and laid out her plan.

As Naomi bundled them into the waiting buggy, Liz phoned the chief. "We need an officer to come to the bakery and pretend to take Emma and her grandson into protective custody."

He balked, but Liz gave him a quick rundown on everything that had transpired in the bakery, conveying the urgency of the situation. He'd already learned from Rhonda that William Purcell was Henry's son and, like Liz, he wasn't sure he believed Henry's intentions in launching the search for his son had been truly benevolent.

Naomi returned from escorting Emma and Timmy to Miriam's waiting buggy and nodded to Liz as she passed the office door.

Thirty seconds later, Liz could hear Henry grilling Naomi about Emma and her grandson. He demanded to be allowed into the back to talk to them.

Naomi refused.

Henry's daughter begged for him to calm down, told him this wasn't the place or time, and warned him he was making a scene.

A moment later, Chief Houghton's voice rose over the others.

Wow, that was fast. Liz drew a deep breath and shook out her limbs. She lifted her chin and walked out to the front of the store.

Stan was talking to Henry. "I've been looking for you. We have your blackmailer in custody. We need you to return to the station and answer some questions."

Henry glanced at his watch. "In custody? How? The meet isn't for another half hour."

"One of your employees upped the time," the chief informed him.

"That's impossible. No one else knew. Not even my secretary." Henry looked to his daughter for confirmation.

Victoria opened her purse and pulled out a bulging envelope. "The money we were going to pay her is still right here."

Henry nodded and she returned the envelope to her purse.

"Chief," Liz said, "Emma's waiting for you in Naomi's office."

"Officer Gerst will take care of her." The chief motioned the young officer, waiting by the door, toward the back of the bakery, then returned his attention to Henry and his daughter. "Could you two please come with me?"

"Wait." Henry lurched after the officer, but the chief caught him by the arm. Henry dug in his heels. "Is he taking Emma somewhere? I need to talk to her." Henry sounded desperate.

An Amish buggy rolled past the front of the store and Liz drew a quick breath, forcing herself to look anywhere but out the window.

But the chief was still tugging Henry in that very direction.

"Chief, wait!" she cried, needing to stall for time.

He looked at Liz impatiently and she scrambled for something to say.

Miriam's buggy passed, and considering how many others meandered through town, maybe the sight wouldn't prompt Henry to think Emma and Timmy had stowed away in one. At least not unless they also happened to see Officer Gerst's diversionary cruiser drive away empty—a risk Liz wasn't willing to take.

"Mr. James has a heart condition," Amy interjected, apparently reading Liz's mind. "You might want to have a doctor check him over before you question him. He's undergone tremendous shock today."

"Yes." Liz flashed Amy a grateful smile.

"There is nothing wrong with me," Henry insisted, "and unless you plan to lay charges, you can't force me to go to the police station before I speak to Emma."

The chief jerked his head toward Officer Gerst's cruiser speeding past the bakery window. "Too late."

Henry covered his face with his hands. "Years too late."

16

"I love Emma," Henry said to Liz as Chief Houghton urged him toward the door of the bakery. "I never stopped loving her. Please, help me. You have to make her understand. I was young and no match for my father. He would've ruined her family, and she would've hated me for it. I had no doubt about that."

"So instead you let her hate you for abandoning her?"

His shoulders slumped. "I don't want her to hate me."

"Why was your father so opposed to her?" Liz asked, ignoring Stan's irritated glance.

"We were college sweethearts." Henry pulled out a chair and looked to the chief for permission to sit.

Stan consented with an impatient sigh.

"My father had never said anything against Emma in our first two years of college. I had no idea he had a problem with her working-class family. Later he'd said he hadn't forbidden the liaison sooner because he thought she'd be one of many college flings. But then, when she told me she was expecting, I told him I was going to marry her. He went ballistic."

Amy quietly pulled out her smartphone and started pressing buttons, no doubt checking to see what she could find out about Henry and his father.

"He forbade the union and made all kinds of threats. I told Emma that maybe we should wait a week or two, to give him time to adjust to the news." Henry shook his head. "At that point, I had no idea what my father was capable of. In his mind, Emma was not a suitable wife and never would be. He went to her behind my back and paid her handsomely to leave. He probably lied to her, saying that I saw how foolish I'd been." Tears filled Henry's eyes. "It wasn't until after Dad died that I found the contract he forced her to sign."

He pounded the table. "It said my son would be provided for as long as his mother never attempted to contact me. Within a month of graduation, my father forced me into an arranged marriage that suited the family's and the business's needs to align themselves with the Duncans."

Henry gave his daughter an apologetic look. "Forgive me. I never loved your mother the way I should have."

Victoria stood stiffly at his side, her expression controlled. She acknowledged his plea with a cool nod.

Liz couldn't blame her. It had to be hard to learn that every time her father had looked at her—as he held her, watched her learn to walk, and heard her greet him with an excited, "Daddy!"—he'd probably been thinking of the son he'd missed those things with.

"We did grow to love each other," Henry reassured Victoria, then added softly, "but it was never like what I'd felt for Emma." His gaze drifted to the front window, looking whimsical. "Still feel. The moment I set eyes on her this afternoon, the old feelings rushed back. It was as if my heart knew her, before my mind even realized who she was. Not that she's changed very much. She's even more beautiful than I remember."

Across the bakery Naomi wore a dreamy smile. Amy too. Liz supposed it was every woman's secret hope there was a man out there who'd feel the same about her—a worthy man.

"I never dared hope we could rekindle that love," Henry went on. "I thought it would be enough to find my son." Henry's face contorted in pain, apparently as the realization that it could never happen hit him afresh.

Henry clutched his chest, and Victoria dropped to her knees at his side. "Daddy, it's going to be okay. I'm here."

"Perhaps we had better take your father to the ER before we go to the station," Stan said.

"That might be best," Henry's daughter agreed.

"He has a history of heart problems?"

"Angina." Victoria clasped her father's arm.

He swatted her away. "The hospital can't help me. I've lost my son without ever being able to meet him. There's no cure for a broken heart."

Naomi quietly set a fresh cup of herbal tea in front of him.

Henry thanked her and took a sip. "I should've started the search sooner. After my wife died two years ago, finding my son was all I could think about, but my father still had controlling interest in the company, so it wasn't until he died six months ago that I could finally act."

Henry planted his elbows on the table and clutched his head. "I was so close. I can't believe William's gone. Who would want to kill him?"

Liz opened her mouth. The chief shot her a cautionary look, but she couldn't *not* ask. Henry was either performing the acting role of his life to cover his own crime, or someone had wanted to make sure he never found his son.

Victoria looked as deeply pained as her father. Her attention was wholly fixed on him, as if she wanted to be hyper alert to the slightest indication he might need medical attention.

"Who else knew about your son?" Liz asked.

This snapped Henry out of his grief. His attention shot to the chief as the reality that someone connected to him might be behind his son's murder seemed to only just dawn on him. "No one," he said.

His forehead scrunched. "Wait, that's not true. My lawyer knows, and the family lawyer before him knew. Other than that, I'm sure my dad would've told as few people as possible. No one who would have any reason to want William dead."

"You are a very wealthy man, are you not?" Amy said. "You control a large multinational company." She must have found that out from the search she'd just done on her phone.

"Yes." The muscles in his jaw flexed as he clearly contemplated other possibilities.

Liz and Amy exchanged glances. Liz saw where her friend was going with her question, so she asked the follow-up. "And once you found your son, naturally, you would've wanted to share all you have with him. Perhaps give him a job in your company?"

Henry nodded. "If he'd been agreeable to it, nothing would've given me greater pleasure."

"Can you think of any business associates who might have been opposed to such a plan? Perhaps fearing it would destabilize the company? Tarnish your reputation?" Amy said.

Henry's lips curled into an inscrutable look. "There are always a few naysayers. It's why I hired Baxter, rather than use the company's private investigators. No one knew of the search except my lawyer."

"I knew," Victoria piped up. "Dad discussed his plans with me at length. I support his decision. I want him to be happy."

Henry reached for his daughter's hand and smiled up at her.

Liz had pegged her as a suspect, since she had the most to lose with her father potentially reinstating a long-lost heir. Yet it seemed unlikely she'd draw attention to her knowledge of his plans if she'd been the one to take advantage of them.

Liz gave Victoria an empathetic smile. "It has to be hard for you—thinking about how the news, when made public, might reflect on your mother's memory and reputation?"

Henry visibly cringed.

A slight tightening around her lips and the flatness in her eyes gave away that it did bother Victoria, but she squeezed her father's hand and repeated, "I want my father to be happy."

Liz nodded. "The chief mentioned you counseled your father to reconsider paying off the blackmailer." She searched Victoria's eyes, attempting to discern if her motive had been more to protect the family from uncontrolled disclosure to the media than to gain information.

"Yes," Victoria said. "At least until we had the facts. Once Dad was ready to go public, of course, the blackmailer would have no further hold over him."

"Wouldn't going public have been the quickest means of locating Emma, and therefore her son?" Amy asked.

Henry shook his head. "My father forced Emma to sign a nondisclosure contract. And after the things my father must've said to her about my feelings for her, I doubt she would've wanted me to find our son."

"It also would have brought out a parade of impostors hoping to cash in on Dad's desire to meet his son," Victoria added.

"Okay," the chief said, helping Henry to his feet and putting an end to the discussion. "We need to finish this at the station. Naomi here has a business to run. And I'm sure Liz needs to get back to her inn."

"Miss Eckhart, please," Henry begged. "Please tell Emma I never stopped loving her. Please tell her I would never do anything to hurt her or our"—he gulped hard—"grandson. He *is* William's son, isn't he?"

Liz didn't answer him, but her face must have betrayed the answer.

"I knew it," he said. "Please, I know she has no reason to trust me after all that has happened, but if she'd give me a second chance, I'd do everything in my power to make it up to her." He drew in a ragged breath. "I can't bring back our son. I know that, but . . . please, *please* convince her to speak with me again."

"I'll see what I can do," she said.

As the door closed behind the group, Amy shimmied out of the booth and scooped up Beans's leash. "You think Henry deserves a second chance."

Liz shrugged. "I have an easier time forgiving his lack of backbone as a young man against his domineering father than the time he waited between the death of his wife and his father to launch the search."

"According to his father's obituary, he'd had heart trouble for a number of years. Henry was probably hoping he wouldn't hold on as long as he did."

"Exactly. So he wouldn't have to finally stand up to him." Liz frowned. "What are the chances Henry's father was taking the heart medicine used to poison William and John?"

"Pretty good. And Henry's father lived with Henry and Victoria in the family mansion."

"You found that online too?" Amy had some serious investigation skills, not that Liz was surprised.

Amy nodded. "Which meant Henry, Victoria, and any other close family associate or servant had access to the leftovers."

"I can't believe Henry would want to hurt his son," Naomi chimed in.

"Me either," Amy said. "I think you were on to something with the business-associate angle. Because we know it was a man, not Victoria, who paid off Rhonda for the information she pilfered from John's room. I thought maybe Victoria might have a fiancé or something with a vested interest in helping her remain the sole heir to the family fortune, but if the online tabloids can be believed, she isn't even dating."

With the chief's cruiser gone, people streamed into the shop.

"We should go," Liz said and took the leash from Amy. Her finger came away tacky. "Yuck. When I grabbed the guy's coat, I got pine gum on my hand and must've gotten some on the leash's handle too." Staring at her fingers, she pressed them together, feeling the stickiness and remembered experiencing the same after cutting spruce branches to decorate the inn. "From the corn knife," she said aloud.

"Huh?" Amy held open the shop door for Liz and Beans.

Excitement welled in Liz's chest as they headed back to the inn. "When we were cutting evergreen boughs, I got sap on my hands and presumably on the corn knife handle. The blade for sure would've had sap on it. Right?"

"Ri–ight." Amy clearly wasn't following Liz's train of thought.

"That guy who paid off Rhonda must've been the one who stole my corn knife from the inn. He could've easily walked out with it hidden under his coat."

"And it would've left the coat sticky," Amy finished.

"Exactly."

"But you didn't recognize him? He wasn't one of your guests?"

"No." Liz scanned the inn's parking lot and, seeing no sign of Gloria's car, held open the front door of the inn for Beans and Amy. "But he could've been that guy who came looking for Gloria. Remember?"

"Absolutely."

"There's more. When Emma and I were walking to the bakery, she recalled a woman with a chow chow yelling at Purcell after a past dog show."

Amy gasped. "Gloria said her husband had had a heart condition before he died."

"Exactly." Something about Gloria had made Liz uneasy from the beginning. "And as a nurse, she'd know how to use his leftover medicine to poison someone."

Amy tugged Liz into the library and said in a hushed voice, "So you think her insulin scheme was just a story to throw us off?"

"Maybe. Although she didn't attempt to hide her distaste for Purcell's judging biases." Liz's excitement flagged as doubts crept in. "Come to think of it, we also have her to thank for spotting Rhonda in the parking lot outside the dog show."

"Sure, but if Rhonda can be believed," Amy countered, "she didn't have anything to do with poisoning John and William. Gloria could simply have decided that she made a good scapegoat."

"Except John said a son was in danger *after* learning William was dead, so he must have been talking about William's son. What motive could Gloria have for taking out her beef with a loathed judge on his son, now that said judge is dead?"

"Maybe Timmy isn't in danger," Amy said. "We only have John's warning to go by. Maybe John assumed that William's killer was someone with a stake in Henry's estate or company, when really he was targeted because of his judging."

Liz shook her head. "It doesn't explain why John was attacked. If only he was lucid enough to tell us who he thinks is after the boy. It has to be someone financially threatened by Henry's secret coming out."

"Maybe Gloria is tied more closely to the James family than we realize."

Beans plopped down in front of Liz and whined. Liz squatted down and searched for the hidden fasteners holding on his costume. Finding them, she helped him out of the Santa suit. He sighed in relief.

"Does your police force have a sketch artist?" Amy asked. "I could probably come up with a decent likeness for the guy who came here looking for Gloria."

"I'm not sure, but that could help."

Sadie poked her head in the door. "There you are. I thought I heard you come in. I just got off the phone with Caitlyn at the hospital. Your Mr. Baxter is awake."

Liz sprang to her feet and gave Sadie a bear hug. "Thank you. Let's go," Liz said to Amy, dropping Beans' costume on the nearest chair. "John should be able to tell us who's behind all of this."

"You think so?" Amy didn't sound nearly as enthusiastic. "If the culprit thought that, he'd be doing everything he or she could to ensure he didn't talk."

Liz's heart missed a beat at that possibility. "The chief should have someone guarding his room."

"I don't think your local police force has enough manpower for that kind of thing."

Liz hurried outside and motioned Amy into the car. "Henry and Victoria could've easily finished John off this morning and didn't. So I guess that's one more thing that suggests they're not involved." Liz stomped on the gas.

"Could just mean they know John has no clue who tried to kill him. Or no proof anyway."

"Well, if he can tell us where to look, we can find the proof."

17

Liz's heart jumped to her throat at the sight of John Baxter lying in his hospital bed, his face as pale as the sheets except for the deep purple caverns beneath his eyes.

Amy set the flowers they'd picked up for him in the hospital gift shop on his night table, then squeezed his hand. "It's so good to see you awake." Her voice cracked. "You had us really worried."

He seemed to drink in the sight of her, color rising to his cheeks. "I'm sorry I missed our dinner."

Liz's gaze jumped to Amy, who smiled and said, "We can reschedule when you're feeling up to it."

Liz blinked. He and Amy had had dinner plans? Amy would've had even more reason than Liz to be worried about his not returning to the inn. No wonder she couldn't believe he didn't choose to disappear.

"Do you know who did this to you?" Liz asked gently.

John sighed, sounding as if the effort pained him. "I don't." He pressed a button that raised the head of his bed. "I take it you've figured out I'm a PI?"

"Yes."

He searched Amy's eyes, his thumb stroking the back of her hand still cradled in his. "I was going to tell you at dinner."

She settled into a chair at his side and smiled encouragingly.

"I'm afraid I've made a few enemies in my line of work." He winced, maybe contemplating another scenario—one where Amy had been in the car too.

Suddenly Liz didn't like the idea of Amy dating this guy.

"How's Peanut?" John whispered.

"His owner came and claimed him."

John nodded. "Sorry for all the trouble."

"That's not important now." She didn't want to overtax him, but for Timmy's sake, she needed some answers. "After I found you in your car and told you Purcell was dead, you said 'son in danger.' Were you talking about his son, Timmy?"

"Purcell's dead?" John rubbed his forehead, his eyes squinting, as if he were straining to pull up the memory.

Liz's heart twisted. She hadn't intended to cause him an additional shock.

Amy shot Liz a concerned look.

"Do you remember meeting with him?" Liz asked gently. "After you asked me to watch Peanut?"

"Yes, but he was fine when I left him." Anguish darkened John's eyes. "What happened?"

"He was poisoned. You both were."

The color drained from his face once more.

"He died soon after leaving the bar. And your car went off the road. It was a full day before we found you."

"May I get you a glass of water?" Amy asked.

"I'm okay," he reassured her and returned his attention to Liz. "I said Timmy was in danger?"

"Well, you didn't use his name; you just said 'son.'"

"I was looking for a client's son."

"Yes, Henry James's, we know. But you said 'son in danger' after I told you Purcell was dead."

John shook his head. "I must've thought my accident and his death were connected. Whoever was behind William's murder would've figured that with me dead, no one would find out Henry had a son."

His hands clenched the sheets. "But if the creep learned William had a son, he'd want to ensure Henry didn't find him either."

"Try to relax," Amy said softly.

Liz's heart squeezed, but they were still no closer to knowing who Timmy might be in danger from. "Do you know who would want to stop the revelation that Henry had a son?"

"No idea. Presumably someone who didn't want the status quo changed—business associates or future beneficiaries." John pushed himself higher in the bed, suddenly looking as determined to get to the bottom of this as Liz. "How long ago did William die?"

"Forty-eight hours, give or take."

"Two days? Whoever was behind this is bound to have heard by now that he was survived by a son."

"Did you tell Henry you'd found William?" Liz asked.

John squinted, as if digging through his memory banks. "No. Not that I recall. But I remember feeling as if I was being followed the first afternoon at the dog show."

Amy grimaced. "That could've been us. We were trying to catch up to you after Peanut flubbed his tracking trial."

John smiled at her, seeming to momentarily forget the gravity of their conversation.

Liz cleared her throat.

John pressed his fingers to his forehead and rubbed, his expression pained. "You said Purcell and I were both poisoned? Was it at the bar?"

"That's our operating theory," Liz confirmed. "It was the only time the two of you were together."

Amy gently filled in details about the corn knife being taken from the inn and used to stab Purcell after he was already dead, and the evidence that John's car had been forced off the road.

"There was a woman in the bar when you were there with Purcell,"

Liz said. "Did you see her?"

John's eyes closed.

"John?" Amy hovered over him. "You still with us?"

"Yeah, just trying to picture the scene. I vaguely remember a woman coming in after us. Had on a black jacket and black knitted winter hat with a large visor." He opened his eyes and looked at Liz. "I didn't see her face. She sat at the bar."

"Could it have been Rhonda Piper?"

He frowned. "I know the woman loathes me, but I don't think she'd kill a stranger just to get to me. Besides I'm sure I would've recognized her if it had been."

Liz didn't bother asking if it had been Gloria. She didn't look like someone who frequented a gym, as the bartender described, and Liz doubted she'd leave the inn without her dog. "How about Victoria James?"

"I haven't met Miss James. I've seen pictures though. And the woman in the bar was in a totally different class."

"What do you mean?" Amy asked.

"No makeup. Cheap dye job. Off-the-rack clothes."

Liz sighed at the newest dead end, because John was right—that description didn't fit Victoria at all. Her makeup was meticulously polished. Her hair model-worthy and her clothes were all designer fashions.

"How well do you know Henry James? Do you think he could've bribed the bartender or waitress to spike your drinks?" Liz asked.

John sighed. "Anything is possible, I guess. But I never got any bad vibes from the guy. If I'd thought for a second he had a morbid motive for wanting me to locate his son, I never would've taken the case."

"Of course you wouldn't," Amy said with a confidence that belied their short acquaintance.

John's eyes slid shut and he seemed to drift off to sleep.

A nurse appeared at the door. "Time for your next dose of pain meds, John."

His eyes fluttered open and a smile lit his face when his gaze met Amy's. Liz moved out of the nurse's way so he could check John's IV.

"You should go now," Amy whispered to Liz. "I'm going to stay with him awhile."

———— *//////////////////////////////* ————

By the time Liz arrived at the inn, having called Mary Ann for a ride home, Sarah had set out afternoon refreshments for the guests. She met Liz in the foyer. "A Henry James and his daughter are here. I gave them tea and asked if they wouldn't mind waiting until you returned."

"Thank you, Sarah. Would you pack up Mr. Baxter's things and bring them down to my quarters? He won't be back for a while from the hospital. And make up the Somewhere in Time Room and the Rose of Sharon Room for the Jameses?"

Liz strolled into the dining area unobserved, since everyone present—Gloria, Edward, Henry, Victoria, Sadie, and Mary Ann—were hunched over the table looking at a slew of photographs spread over the entire surface.

Liz poured herself a cup of tea, then joined them. "Are these from the dog show?"

Sadie laid out a few more. "I decided to make prints of all of them in case any of your guests wanted some."

Liz gave them only a cursory glance, not wanting to miss her chance. "Henry, do you know Gloria?" Liz said, as if it were a given.

Henry nodded to the woman. "Yes, she introduced herself when we arrived." Neither his tone nor his expression betrayed any hint he was lying.

Liz glanced from Gloria to Victoria, but neither woman seemed flustered by Liz's question either. Maybe Gloria had no connection to the family after all, other than hating Henry's estranged son. Maybe Timmy wasn't in danger. Maybe Gloria had killed William and that was the end of it.

Except if she had done it, why poison John's drink too? Why run him off the road? She wouldn't have known what he was investigating. Not to mention she hadn't been in the bar and didn't drive a black car—unlike the man with the evergreen sap on his coat who had paid off Rhonda for John's tablet.

Edward finished off his cup of tea and then picked up a photo of himself with his shih tzu. "Do you mind if I keep this one?"

"Not at all," Sadie said, sounding pleased he'd found one he wanted. "That's why I brought them."

Gloria chose a couple from the grand parade, then wandered out with Edward and Mary Ann. Henry, however, continued to scrutinize the photos.

"May we check in now?" Victoria asked Liz.

"Absolutely." Liz rose along with Victoria, but her father hadn't even seemed to hear.

"I'll take care of it," Victoria said to her father and followed Liz to the reception desk, where she filled out the paperwork.

Amy came in, her cheeks rosy. "John was still—" She cut herself off when she saw Victoria.

"Hello," Victoria said to her. She took the key from Liz and returned to the dining room.

"I hope you don't mind," Liz said. "I gave them the room that was going to go to you."

"That's okay. I just didn't want to say anything about John in front of her. Even knowing they hired him, I don't like how they were snooping through his stuff when we found them in his hospital room."

"How's he doing?" Liz asked, unable to rein in the smile that crept to her lips.

"Sleeping, and he looked as if he would be for a while."

"Why didn't you tell me you two had a dinner date the other night?"

Amy mirrored her grin and shrugged. "I guess I didn't know what to think when he didn't show up. I didn't want to tell you that one of your guests stood me up."

They walked to the dining room. Sadie had gathered up all but a couple dozen photos. "I'll come back for whatever is left once we close up shop," she said and left the stack on the table beside the ones Henry was still frowning at.

"These are from the afternoon before William was killed," he said to Liz. "Do you see him in any of these? I'm afraid I wouldn't recognize him."

Liz sat beside him and dutifully studied the photos. "No, I'm sorry. I don't see him. He took ill after breakfast that morning, so he probably wasn't even at the fairgrounds building at the time these photos were taken. But I can show you a picture of him." She slipped out to her private quarters and grabbed the dog show program from her purse. Striding back into the dining room, she opened the program to the spread of judges' photos. She set it in front of Henry and pointed to William's photo. "That's him."

Victoria looked at it over Henry's shoulder. "Wow, he looked a lot like you."

Henry blinked rapidly. "I was so close. I missed him by mere days." He fished a tissue out of his pocket and blew his nose, then swiped at his eyes with the back of his hand. "If I hadn't hired John, he might still be alive."

Victoria squeezed her father's shoulder. "You don't know that. You mustn't blame yourself."

Henry surged to his feet, his gaze fixed on Liz. "Please, could you invite Emma here? Convince her to see me. I need her to know I never meant William any harm. I want to meet my grandson and maybe become a part of his life. I don't blame Emma for hating me, but I'll do whatever I can to help her."

"What if what she wants is for you to leave her and her grandson alone?"

Henry's expression crumbled. He paced the room, shaking his head. He pounded his fist against the fireplace mantel, then dropped his head to it. After a long moment, he turned back to Liz. "I know I don't deserve it, but please, convince her to give me a second chance. I couldn't bear to be shut out of my grandson's life."

Suspicions and doubts wrestled with too many other emotions in Liz's heart. She started gathering the dishes. "Why don't you and your daughter settle into your rooms now and I'll see what I can do."

Henry's face brightened. "Thank you so much! I can't describe what that means to me."

Amy helped Liz clear the table.

Once Henry and Victoria were safely upstairs, Liz said, "Could you keep an eye on everyone here for me while I slip over to Miriam's to speak to Emma?"

"Sure. No problem."

"Thank you. I'll be back as soon as I can." Liz hurriedly stuffed her arms into her coat. "Call me if anyone leaves the inn or does anything suspicious."

Amy's expression turned wary. "Are you sure about this?"

Liz pulled on her gloves and grabbed her car keys. "I'm not sure about anything. But I do know how it feels to suddenly find out you have more family than you ever imagined and to burn with the longing to meet them."

"What if Henry is playing on your sympathies to get close to Emma for darker reasons?"

Liz wavered on the inn's threshold and searched Amy's gaze.

Her friend had been a criminal lawyer—and a good one—for years. If anyone could tell when a man like Henry James was lying, it would be Amy. "Is that what you think he's doing?"

Amy let out a long sigh. "No. He seems sincere. But we don't know anything about the other people who might be privy to whatever information he gains—household staff, his secretary, his lawyer, his daughter. I'm not confident we can trust the people he might trust."

Liz nodded. She'd had the same thought. "Well, there's no harm in my talking to Emma. Ultimately, the choice will be hers."

Amy crossed her arms over her chest as if warding off a chill. "Be careful."

"I will." Liz closed the door behind her.

Two blocks from the inn, Liz caught sight of a black sedan in her rearview mirror, and an uneasy feeling rippled through her. She passed the road that would have taken her to her cousin's farm and took a fast right onto a street that circled through a residential area and came back out onto the road a block farther along.

She slowed as she drove around the circle and pulled up at the intersection. The black car should have either followed her, or passed by the intersection. But it wasn't behind her or off to her right.

She glanced to her left and saw it. The black sedan was parked eight car lengths back, partially hidden behind an old pickup.

Her heart skipped a beat. This was no coincidence. She turned right and headed for the grocery store, her gaze straying to the rearview mirror every few seconds.

The black sedan didn't reappear.

Liz parked in the grocery store lot and debated what to do. Without the sedan in sight, there was no point in calling the police. But should she risk driving to see Emma and potentially leading a murderer to her grandson?

Liz climbed out of her car and scanned the streets flanking the parking lot. No black sedan in sight. Just in case the driver was somehow still watching her, she went into the grocery store to make it look as if a quick shopping trip had been her intent all along. She picked up a dozen eggs, a loaf of bread, and a carton of milk, then meandered back outside carrying her sack of groceries.

A black sedan was now parked in the far corner of the lot. No driver inside.

She surreptitiously scouted the area as she hurried toward her car. An ambulance whirred past, momentarily snagging her attention. But then as she climbed into her car, she glimpsed a man in his mid-fifties wearing a dark overcoat and limping toward the black sedan. Limping on his left leg. Beans had bitten the guy who'd paid off Rhonda on his left leg. Liz pulled her cell phone from her purse and slid her finger across the screen to wake it up.

Nothing happened.

"No! You can't be dead now!"

18

If she ran back into the grocery store to use the phone, it'd only raise his suspicions. She started her car and turned out of the parking lot in the direction of Jackson's furniture factory and showroom.

As expected, the black sedan waited for a couple of cars to pass, then pulled out behind her.

Both cars between them turned off before she reached Jackson's furniture store, and the black sedan fell further behind. But Liz wasn't fooled. She turned into the store lot and parked in front of the door. Aside from a couple of employee vehicles, the lot was empty, which would make it impossible for the sedan to blend in. Liz sat in her car, her gaze fixed on the rearview mirror.

Thirty seconds passed. Then a minute.

Had he pulled over before reaching the store? She squinted out the side window, but couldn't see the sedan.

"I'm not being paranoid," she muttered.

Jackson poked his head out the shop's front door. "Good to see you, Liz. Coming in?"

Liz hiked her purse strap over her shoulder and climbed out of her car. "Can you see a black sedan down the street?" Liz asked, not wanting to look and let on to the driver that she'd spotted him.

"The one behind the green van?" Jackson held the door open for her.

She slipped inside. "Can you see the license plate? And do you have a way to charge my phone?"

"No front plates." Jackson released the door. "There's a charging cable behind the counter. What's going on?"

"We need to call the chief." She caught Jackson up on Henry James's connection to their murder victim and what had gone down with Rhonda at the fairgrounds that afternoon. "I'm sure this is the same guy. I have no idea who he is or why he wouldn't want Henry to find his son, but I think he's killer and somehow he figured out I know where Emma and her grandson are hiding. I'm sure he's hoping I'll lead him to her."

"Or maybe he's someone Henry hired to find his son's killer?" Jackson speculated.

Liz let herself behind the counter in the middle of the store and plugged her phone into the promised cable. "Only if he lied about who paid off Rhonda, because this is definitely the same guy. May I use your shop phone to call the chief?"

"You want the police to arrest him for buying stolen property? Because a sticky coat isn't enough to indict him for Purcell's murder, especially when the knife wound was inflicted after Purcell was already dead."

"If he's off the street, he can't hurt Henry's grandson. And once the news is out, he'll have no reason to."

"Assuming that's his motive."

Liz twisted the phone cord between her fingers. If Victoria had hired him to do her dirty work so she wouldn't have to share her inheritance, she'd just go looking for another lackey—and probably have this guy killed before he could give her up.

The chief finally picked up.

Liz put the phone on speaker so Jackson could hear and repeated her suspicions about the guy outside. As she spoke, one of Jackson's employees came in. Jackson said something Liz didn't hear to the employee, who nodded and left again.

"I'll be right there," the chief said when she finished her tale.

"No wait. I was thinking if we play this right, we might be able to catch him attempting to go after Timmy."

Jackson's concerned look grew even darker.

"We can't risk the boy's safety," Stan said.

"Of course not. But this guy doesn't know where Emma and her grandson are, right? Or he would already be there, not following me. How about if I lead him to a setup?" Liz said.

"A setup?"

"The old Ferguson cottage," Jackson said thoughtfully. "You and your men can set up an ambush. We'll make it look as if Emma and the boy are hiding out there."

"We'll show up with a bag of groceries," Liz said.

"I can't put you two in danger either."

"I suspect he'd wait until after we left the cottage before making a move—watch the place for a while and wait for nightfall. But either way, if your men are ready for him, he won't be able to get away with anything." Liz thought this could work.

"I appreciate your confidence in our abilities, but it'd take time to assess the options and get a tactical team in position."

"How long do you need, Stan?" Jackson asked.

"This guy isn't playing around," Stan said. "After my officer left the bakery for his make-believe recovery of Emma and her grandson, he retrieved her car. The brakes had been cut."

Liz gulped, envisioning what could've happened if she hadn't invited Emma and Timmy for tea and cupcakes.

"All the more reason to stop him. How long do you need?" Jackson repeated.

"An hour at least. I need twenty minutes just to get my team suited up and over there. And I've got to clear it with the Fergusons. They're in Florida."

"I'll drive with Liz, so he won't be tempted to make his move until after we leave," Jackson said.

One of Jackson's employees came in via the back door and handed him a slip of paper. Jackson glanced at it, then said to the chief, "I've got a license plate number for you on this guy."

Liz perked up at the news. She'd seen Jackson say something to his employee while she'd been on the phone, but had never imagined he'd sent him out to spy for them.

After Jackson read off the number, Stan thanked him and hung up.

"How long a drive is that cottage from here?" Liz asked.

"Ten minutes. Although I could take a circuitous route that'd drag it out to twenty or more." He consulted his watch. "That still leaves us with forty minutes to kill. I'm not sure he'll stick around that long unless we give him something to whet his appetite."

Liz considered. "What did you have in mind?"

"You stopped for groceries, presumably for Emma and her grandson. So why would you stop at a furniture store?"

"For furniture."

"Exactly. Is the boy young enough to need a crib?"

"No."

Jackson glanced around the store. "Well, we could load up some bedding at least. Maybe stop by the hardware store and pick up a small TV and DVD player, some kids games or movies. That'll convince him you're heading out to visit the pair and easily kill forty minutes."

"Great idea." Liz grabbed her phone.

Jackson pulled two pillows, the sheets, and the comforter off one of his display beds, then led the way out.

Liz unlocked her car and shifted the groceries in the trunk to make room for the bedding.

"Why don't you grab those and we'll put everything in my truck?"

Jackson suggested. "It has a lot more power if we need to make a quick getaway. And I have another charging cable in there so you can keep charging your phone."

Her heart thumped and she stole a glance down the street. She could just make out the front fender of the sedan, poking out past the green van. "Its parking light is broken," she murmured.

Jackson opened the rear door of his pickup's cab. "Is that significant?"

"They think the car that nudged John's off the road broke a light in the process." Her stomach did a slow roll at the prospect of a repeat performance, only with Jackson's truck.

They drove to the hardware store.

"I don't see him. Do you?" Jackson asked as they headed inside.

A black sedan rounded the corner at the end of the block.

"There." Liz pretended not to notice it and pushed through the door. Fifteen minutes later they emerged with a TV, a DVD player, and a couple movies. The sedan had driven past the store and parked up the street.

Jackson discreetly texted the chief. A moment later, his phone beeped and Jackson checked the screen. "He says give them twenty more minutes."

"We can drive slowly," Liz said.

Jackson opened the door for her. "There's still time to change your mind. I could drive this stuff out myself."

"No way. I'm in."

"Okay, let's do it." Jackson drove a circuitous route to the isolated cabin.

Liz scrutinized her side mirror. "Do you see him?"

"He's back there. Every once in a while he slips into view."

Jackson flipped on his signal as the cottage's overgrown driveway came into view a hundred yards ahead of them. He took his time slowing down for the turn. "There he is," he said and swung into the driveway.

Liz took a deep breath. "I hope he decides to wait for us to leave before making his move."

"With everything we're bringing to the cabin, he'll feel confident Emma and her boy won't move anytime soon." Jackson parked in front of the door.

The curtains at the cabin's windows were all closed, but a light could be seen inside. The cabin's clapboard siding was gray and sagging. Fallen leaves overflowed the gutters. One set of tire tracks indented the grassy driveway, but there was no car in sight.

"Thank goodness there's no snow on the ground, or the cops would never have been able to hide their tracks," Liz said. She climbed out of the car and took in the cabin. The cozy smell of a fireplace wafted to her nose. Wisps of smoke drifted from the cabin's chimney.

"They did a good job of making the place look occupied," Jackson said, hoisting the TV out of the back.

Liz grabbed the bedding and glanced around the small clearing.

A twig snapped in the woods behind her.

One of the officers? Or was it their man sneaking up to spy on them already? Liz's pulse shifted into double time. "Did you hear that?" she whispered.

Jackson moved between her and the direction of the sound. "Get inside."

What if the cabin's isolation emboldened this guy to make a brazen move? Dusk was already settling in. She knocked on the door then tried the knob.

It turned beneath her fingers and Stan quickly ushered them inside.

"We heard a twig snap in the woods south of the driveway," Jackson said, setting down the boxes. "One of your men?"

"Nope. They're in tree stands east and west of the house and behind it." He pulled his radio from his shoulder and depressed the talk button. "Hughes, report in."

"No sign of anyone yet," his response came back.

"Watch south of the driveway," Stan ordered, then turned to Jackson. "You two had better get going."

As much as Liz wanted to do exactly that, she shook her head. "He might get suspicious if we don't stay long enough to set up the TV for Emma and visit awhile. I'll grab the groceries and movies from the car," Liz said as Jackson pulled the TV from its box.

"Hold it." Stan beat her to the door. "I'll escort you."

"You want him to know you're here?"

"You bet I do. We wouldn't leave Emma at a safe house without protection. He's got to be counting on that." Into his radio, Stan said, "We're coming out."

"Ten-four," the officers responded.

The chief drew his weapon and slowly opened the door, peering around it. Seemingly satisfied, he motioned Liz to follow him down the porch steps to Jackson's truck. He kept Liz between him and the house or him and the truck the entire time as he continuously scanned the area.

Liz handed Stan the DVD player and then scooped up the grocery and movie bags and hurried back inside.

Stan paused on the porch, his back to the house and scanned the woods beyond the clearing. "Going back inside," he said into his radio. "Report in." He joined Jackson and Liz and locked the door.

"No movement on the east side," Officer Gerst came back.

"Hughes?" the chief asked.

No response.

The chief must've interpreted Liz's sharp intake of breath as fear for him, because he reassured her in a soft voice, "He may have turned down his radio volume if he spotted our guy approaching, or may not want to risk being overheard responding."

"Dixon?" the chief hissed into the radio.

"Clear."

Stan snatched up a pair of binoculars and edged aside the curtain in the southeast corner. "You two better get going. It'll be dark soon." He opened the door, scanned the area, and then slipped out ahead of them. "Okay, go."

Liz and Jackson hurried into the truck. The chief stood watch on the porch as Jackson backed up and spun the truck around to head out the long driveway. Trees flanked either side, leafless, but thick enough to cut off what was left of the twilight.

About a hundred yards from the road, someone sprang up from behind Jackson's seat and pressed a gun to his neck. "Stop the truck."

Jackson did as he was told.

The guy pulled the trigger. Liz screamed.

19

Jackson's entire body went into convulsions and he slumped on the seat.

"Shut up," his attacker snarled at Liz. "Or you're next."

Liz fell silent, feeling frantically for her seat-belt button.

Jackson had stopped convulsing on the truck seat beside her, but was clearly struggling to shake off the stun gun's effects.

Still struggling to break free of her seat belt, Liz twisted around to face their assailant, who wore a ski mask. "Who are you? What do you want?"

He threaded handcuffs through the steering wheel and snapped them onto Jackson's hands. "How many cops are inside?" he growled, reloading his stun gun.

"One," she said loudly, trying to cover the click of her seat-belt clasp. She shimmied backward toward the truck door, feeling behind her for the handle.

"And outside? How many?" he pressed.

Her fingers found the door handle. "One!" She tumbled out of the truck and sprinted for the clearing. "Help!" she screamed.

A sharp barb caught her in the shoulder.

She yanked it out on the run, thankful the second one had missed her body, failing to close the circuit.

Liz saw Stan take cover behind a porch pillar. He held a gun and wore goggles, probably night-vision. It was hard to tell in the deepening twilight. "Liz?"

"He used a stun gun on Jackson!" Liz shouted, running like a madwoman toward him.

Sirens erupted in the distance. Liz hoped it was police cars maneuvering to block the roads if her assailant did the smart thing and tried to retreat. Her step faltered at the sudden thought of what else he might do—perhaps take Jackson hostage to fight his way out.

Stan reached out his hand and tugged her up the stairs. "Just one guy?"

"Yes."

"Get inside."

Liz rushed in and the chief grabbed the door handle. "Stay away from the windows," he warned, then yanked the door shut, leaving her alone inside.

Her heart rioted. She switched off the LED lanterns spaced around the room and then ran to peer through the front window. She could just make out the chief and two of his officers sweeping the area from the cabin toward Jackson's truck. That left one officer still guarding the rear.

This was so not how she'd thought this would go down. *Please let the police catch this guy!* She slinked over to the side window and pulled back a curtain just far enough to see outside without giving away her position. The moonless sky was now black. She could barely make out individual trees beyond the clearing, let alone someone hiding amongst them.

A scratching noise whispered from the back of the cabin. Was it one of the cops checking the perimeter? A squirrel searching for a winter home? The bad guy?

Liz ducked into the kitchen area and grabbed the cast-iron frying pan sitting on the stove.

The sound came again. A tree branch scraping against the side of the cabin, maybe? The roar of blood pounding in Liz's ears made it impossible to pinpoint the origin. *Calm down. The bad guy's not stupid enough to attempt to grab the boy right out from underneath the cops' noses. How would he get away?*

Then again, most of Pleasant Creek's cops were already here. Unless the captain had alerted state troopers to assist with roadblocks—

The back door creaked open and Liz crouched behind a cupboard, clutching the frying pan's handle.

A dark figure padded inside, his gun leading the way. "Where are you?" he whispered hoarsely. "The chief asked me to sneak you out the back."

In the scant light, Liz couldn't make out his face, except that he wore the same kind of night-vision goggles as Stan had and not a black ski mask. "How do you know the guy hasn't circled around back?"

He lowered his gun arm. "They've got him surrounded in front."

Liz didn't recognize his voice, probably thanks to his hushed tone, but that didn't stop her palm from growing slick with sweat as she tightened her grip on the pan.

He took a single step toward her. "Come on."

She held the frying pan out of view behind her and stood.

"Where are the other two?" he asked urgently.

Her heart ricocheted off her ribs.

This guy wasn't one of the chief's men. They all knew this was a sting operation, that Emma and her grandson weren't really here. And if Stan had sent a state trooper in after her, he'd have told the guy she was the only one in here.

"In the bedroom," she whispered, barely finding enough air to be heard. "The boy's sleeping on the bed," she added. "You'll have to carry him."

"No problem. Follow me." As she'd hoped, he turned toward the bedroom and pocketed his gun, because he had no holster. She hoped it wasn't a gun either, just the same stun gun he'd had outside.

Liz didn't want to get close enough to find out. As he padded toward the bedroom, she beelined for the front door—where the real officers were.

"Not that way," the guy whispered, apparently still thinking she believed him.

She stopped and, keeping the frying pan out of his line of sight, slowly turned. The second he saw the empty bed in that room, he'd know the truth. She probably should've kept going and gotten out while she could. Her mind scrambled through options as she looked up at his goggle-clad face, what she could make out of it in the dark at least. "Sorry. The darkness has me all disoriented."

That's it! She felt her way to the end table and grabbed the flashlight she'd seen on it, before dousing the lights.

"What are you doing?"

"This." She flicked on the light and pointed it at his night-vision goggles.

He let out a curse and turned his head away, his arm lifting to block the beam.

She sprang forward, aiming the frying pan at his head. Thanks to his height advantage, his shoulder took the brunt of the hit. She raced for the door and yanked on the knob.

It didn't give.

She fumbled with the lock.

Two sharp jabs caught her in the leg, which convulsed uncontrollably.

"Help!" she screamed and lurched for the front window, swinging the frying pan at it. "He's in here!" she shouted over the sound of shattering glass, then collapsed to the floor.

Footsteps pounded up the porch stairs, and she managed to roll out of the way of the door a second before one of the real officers kicked it open. Stan squatted at her side as shouts of "Clear!" burst out from other parts of the cabin. "You okay?" he asked.

She yanked the barbs from her leg, grateful he'd only succeeded in immobilizing it. "I will be when you catch that guy. He had on night-vision goggles and was pretending to be one of your men." She pushed herself to her hands and knees, and spotted the tip of a shoe poking out from behind the couch. He must be hiding between the couch and the wall. She caught Stan's pant leg as he stepped away, speaking to his men.

He glanced down at her and she pointed to the couch. "Does he have a gun?" Stan asked.

"I only saw a stun gun."

"Flick the rest of those lights on," Stan said. Then he silently motioned to his men to surround the couch. With all guns aimed at the couch, Stan grabbed the couch and heaved it away from the wall.

"Freeze!" the men shouted as one.

The guy raised his arms in surrender.

Stan pushed him onto his stomach with his boot and another officer searched him—handing Stan his stun gun and wallet. Then he handcuffed him, hauled him to his feet, and tore off the night-vision goggles.

"You recognize him?" Stan asked Liz.

"Yeah, he's the one who paid Rhonda for John's tablet. If you check his car, you'll probably find his overcoat with sticky pine residue on the inside."

The guy's forehead wrinkled in confusion.

"It proves you stole the corn knife from my inn," Liz said. "The corn knife you used to stab William Purcell."

The man's face blanked. "I have no idea what you're talking about."

She didn't buy that. The evidence was circumstantial, she knew, but compelling. "We have a witness who can place you at the inn." Liz had only seen him from behind, but Amy had spoken to him. "You claimed you were looking for Gloria Hunt. Is she an accomplice? I'm sure she won't hesitate to spill everything she knows in return for leniency the instant she learns of your capture."

He didn't look concerned by that news, which likely meant he'd merely spotted her name on the register and had used visiting her as a convenient excuse when questioned.

A call came in on the chief's radio, saying they'd found the officer who'd been guarding the back of the cabin. Their would-be kidnapper had stunned, gagged, and handcuffed him, then commandeered his night-vision goggles.

The chief thumbed through the guy's wallet and pulled out a driver's license. "Clive Duncan," he read off the card. "You're under arrest for three counts of assault with a weapon."

"Don't forget forcible confinement," Liz added. "He handcuffed Jackson to his steering wheel. And he impersonated an officer. And uttered death threats." It seemed like eons ago, but she was pretty sure he'd threatened their lives back in the truck. "And attempted kidnapping. He came in looking for Emma and her grandson."

"Okay," Stan said in a silencing tone that was not at all like his usual manner. "I'm sure we will have several more charges to lay on Mr. Duncan."

Duncan. Liz mentally replayed Henry James's account of his forced marriage. "Henry's wife was a Duncan," Liz said. She faced her assailant. "Who are you? Her brother?"

From the tightening of his lips and the flicker in his eyes, Liz was pretty sure she'd nailed the connection in one guess. "So that'd make you Victoria's uncle. A beloved uncle, no doubt. The kind of uncle who, like Victoria, wouldn't want her mother's memory desecrated by her father's revelations of a *love* child."

Duncan's lips curled. His face reddened.

"So did the two of you hatch this plan together?"

Stan tugged Liz aside, his voice hushed. "We need to read him his rights before we start interrogating him. You know that." He waved Gerst over. "Help her back to the truck. If Jackson's not up to driving, you can take them both home." To Liz, he added, "We can get your full statements after we finish up here."

Liz didn't want to leave, but she didn't argue. She'd been a lawyer long enough to know her questions could have messed up their ability to secure a conviction. But the flash of panic in Clive's eyes had told her all she needed to know. The trick now was to prove that Victoria was in on his plans.

Dear old Uncle Clive didn't look like the type who'd cave under pressure or who'd sell out his niece to save his own hide. In fact, his best hope of coming out of all of this with anything was if Victoria appeared squeaky clean—the all-deserving beneficiary of her father's fortune. A fortune she'd then be free to share with the uncle who'd made it possible.

As she stepped out of the cabin, Stan came to the door. "By the way," he said, showing her a motel's magnetic key card, "you were right about him staying at the Shady Rest Motel."

Liz grinned. "When you find his car, check the lights."

Stan winked. "You can count on it."

Jackson ran up to Liz as she descended the cabin steps. "Are you okay?"

She rubbed her thigh where the stun gun prongs had hit her. "Yeah, getting zapped in the leg wasn't nearly as brutal as what he did to you."

Jackson winced. "I'm sorry you had to go through that."

"She did good," Officer Gerst said, sounding like a proud papa, even though Liz had more than a few years on him. "We got our guy."

Wrapping his arm around Liz's shoulder, Jackson hugged her to his side. "Can we go home now?"

"Yup, you're free to go."

Liz hadn't realized she was jittery until the solid warmth of Jackson's arm held her still. A quiet peace washed over her as Jackson walked her to his truck, his arm still around her. "Thank you for being here," she said.

He gave her one last tight squeeze, double-checked the area behind her seat for stowaways and then helped her up into the truck. "You've got to get a safer hobby."

"Hobby?"

"Sleuthing. I've lost count of how many mysteries you've solved." Liz rolled her eyes.

Jackson circled the truck and climbed into the driver's seat.

Gerst jogged out to them, toting a hardware store bag. "The chief thought you might want to take these movies for the boy. We'll deliver the television and DVD player to the inn later."

"Thanks." Liz took the bag through the truck window and turned to Jackson. "We should donate our purchases to a charity."

Jackson slung his arm over the back of the seat and backed slowly down the driveway. "Great idea. Emma will be happy to hear it's safe for her and her grandson to head home."

"I'm not so sure." Liz mindlessly flipped through the DVDs. "Only Henry and Victoria knew about the blackmail scheme, besides Rhonda. One of them must have tipped off Clive."

Jackson abruptly braked. "Where are Henry and Victoria now?"

"At the inn."

Jackson's jaw stiffened, and the relief that had been plain on his face after Clive's capture evaporated. "Victoria must have been disturbed to learn she had a half brother her father never told her about. It would've been natural for her to vent about the revelation to her uncle—her mother's brother—without having any ulterior motive."

"Maybe."

"The revelation would've cast a pall over his sister's memory," he continued as he drove them back toward Pleasant Creek. "Goes to Clive Duncan's motive."

"Motive to kill? To risk spending the rest of his life in jail so his deceased sister wouldn't become the butt of a few jokes in poor taste?"

"He didn't think he'd get caught."

"Okay, but Victoria would've been feeling all that too, compounded with the prospect of losing half her fortune to the child of her mother's nemesis. Not to mention that something about the way Victoria was acting this afternoon seemed off."

Jackson's grip tightened on the steering wheel. "Off how?"

"Like in the middle of our major revelation conversation in the bakery, she tuned out and texted someone on her phone." Liz sat up straighter, willing the truck to move faster. "I wish we could check her phone and see if she was texting her uncle."

"You mean to tip him off about Emma and her grandson being taken to a safe house?"

"Exactly." Liz texted the chief to suggest he check Clive's phone. Which he would no doubt do anyway, but she felt better for passing along the thought.

A photo message came in from Sadie of Emma's grandson hugging Beans in the bakery earlier. A mishmash of different boots—Emma's short, low-heeled black ones, Amy's stylish leg-hugging ones, Liz's hikers—were visible under the table in the background. The image triggered a memory of the woman in designer boots who'd been stopped by the dog show's security after attempting to enter the area restricted to competitors and staff—only moments after John had entered.

Had she been following John? Maybe reporting back to Clive?

As the guard questioned her, she'd appeared to be anxious about losing sight of someone. Liz stared at the image of Emma's grandson on her cell phone and shook her head. The dog show was over, and the woman—whoever she was—was probably long gone.

Still, Liz couldn't shake thoughts of the woman, or more precisely, the incongruity of her designer boots and thrift-store wardrobe.

Liz mentally raked through the photos Sadie had spread out on the dining room table earlier. There'd been none of the woman even though Liz remembered Sadie snapping a photo specifically of her. *Someone must've swiped them. And I think I know why.*

20

Liz called Sadie and asked if she could send the picture to Liz's phone. A moment later a photo popped up. Liz's attention went straight to the woman's boots—exactly the kind of boots she'd expect Victoria to wear. Liz scrutinized the woman's profile, ignoring the glaringly different hair color and style, the dramatic makeup, and secondhand clothes no one would ever expect to see worn by a woman as wealthy as Victoria James. "It's her."

Jackson turned into his store's parking lot and stopped next to Liz's car. "Who's her?"

Liz showed him the image on the screen. "This is Victoria James at the dog show."

"And?"

"Don't you see? Look at the time stamp in the bottom corner."

Jackson squinted at the picture, then looked questioningly at Liz.

"It's the day William Purcell was killed. Victoria was *here* the day her half brother was killed. But I guarantee you she didn't admit that to the police chief. She probably fabricated some alibi about being at home in Indianapolis."

"Hmm." Jackson pulled up the Internet on his phone and searched for an image of Victoria. "Here we go. This one was taken at a gala last week." He held the two screens side-by-side and frowned. "I'm not seeing the resemblance."

"Look past the hair color and makeup. Look at the shape of her nose, the pouty bulge of her bottom lip, the stray curl in the middle of her forehead, the crooked dimple at the corner of her mouth."

"I see what you mean. You could be right."

Liz took back her phone. "I know I am. I sensed Victoria was acting cagey at the inn when we were all looking at Sadie's photos from the dog show. I think she palmed this picture so we wouldn't see it and recognize her."

"That's a possibility."

Liz phoned Amy. "Hey, remember the designer boots you admired on that woman at the dog show?"

"Yeah."

"They're the kind of boots a woman like Victoria James would wear, don't you think?"

Amy sounded as if she choked on whatever she'd been eating. "You think that Goth girl was paid off by Victoria?"

"Nope, I think she was Victoria herself. I think she stole the photo Sadie took of her so we wouldn't figure it out."

"Oh, wow. Have you told the police?"

"Not yet. You didn't happen to notice what kind of boots she was wearing today, did you?"

Amy groaned. "No, sorry. But don't worry—I'll be sure to pay attention the next time she comes down. Are you still at your cousin's?"

"I haven't made it there yet. I'll explain when I get back."

"Okay. I'll keep my eyes and ears open," Amy said.

Liz thanked her friend and ended the call.

Jackson shook his head. "You think Victoria would be dumb enough to wear the same boots back to town?"

Liz shrugged. "When I find a pair of boots I love, I wear them everywhere."

"Her shoe budget likely rivals your annual income."

Liz stifled a groan. "Okay, I think we need to pay the bartender who served William and John at Murphy's another visit to see if he recognizes designer-boot girl."

Fifteen minutes later, they arrived at the bar. The parking lot was packed. "This might not be the best time to talk to the bartender," Liz said.

Jackson hopped out of the truck and opened the passenger-side door for her. "We're here now. We may as well try."

They wove their way through the crowds in the dimly lit room toward the bar. "That's him," Liz said. She reminded him who she was and showed him the picture on her phone.

He examined it, looking undecided. "She had a hat on, so I didn't notice any funky colors in her hair. But her makeup was pale like that, and I do remember she had full lips." He showed it to a female server returning an empty tray to the bar. "Does she look like that woman who was here that afternoon?"

The server glanced at the screen. "Yup, that's her," she said without a second's hesitation. "Would recognize the boots anywhere."

Liz refrained from pumping her fist in victory and instead thanked them for their assistance.

Once outside the reality of what the revelation meant hit Liz full bore, and she suddenly felt nauseated.

"Are you okay?" Jackson asked.

"No." Liz's chest felt as if an elephant had plunked down on it. "I mean, I was sure Victoria was involved and that's what I wanted to prove, but if she was in the bar, then that means she was most likely the one who poisoned William and John."

"And stabbed William?"

Liz inhaled a deep breath in a futile attempt to tamp down the woozy feeling. "Clive could have stabbed him as a precaution after the fact. Or to make it look like a mugging or something in hopes the police wouldn't detect the overdose of heart medicine in Purcell's system."

"And he could've forced John off the road for the same reason," Jackson murmured.

"I have a murderer staying at my inn," she said. "Victoria's probably waiting for confirmation from her uncle that Emma's grandson is dead too."

"We'll talk to the chief."

"And if that isn't bad enough, poor Henry now has to face the fact that his efforts to find his son cost his son's life—at his daughter's hand. And who knows if Emma will ever let him see his grandson. Who could blame her?"

Jackson nodded. "Especially if Henry were to put the full power of his wealth behind giving his daughter the best legal defense money can buy."

Liz opened the truck door. "The DA might not even attempt to charge her on such scant circumstantial evidence. Not unless her uncle rats her out."

Jackson climbed in beside Liz and started the truck. "There's got to be a way to get her to confess."

"Or at least to give herself away," Liz murmured, the vague threads of an idea weaving through her mind. "Let's go to Miriam's."

———————————————————

When they reached her cousin's home, Liz laid out her plan.

When they arrived back at the inn an hour later, the house looked warm and welcoming with the Christmas lights shining through the darkness. Liz and Jackson helped Emma and Timmy out of the truck.

Emma looked nervously up at the inn. "Are you sure about this?"

"The two of you once had something very special. If nothing else, talking with Henry might give you the closure his father never allowed."

Emma clutched Timmy's hand and exhaled loudly. "Or it will open a new can of worms?"

Liz exchanged a glance with Jackson, second-guessing her plan. The last thing she wanted to do was cause the grieving woman more pain.

As if he'd read her mind, Jackson coaxed Liz forward and whispered close to her ear, "It's a good plan."

The fragrance of pine boughs greeted them as they pushed through the front door.

Amy, Mary Ann, Sadie, and Beans met them in the foyer.

"Where are Henry and Victoria?" Liz asked.

Amy pulled Beans by the collar to halt the face licking he was giving Emma's grandson. "Takeout pizza arrived for them about forty minutes ago. They've been in their rooms ever since."

Liz helped Timmy out of his coat and then relieved Emma of hers. "Amy will show you to the library while I fetch Henry and his daughter."

Amy asked Sadie and Mary Ann if they would show the Purcells the way to the library instead and then tugged Liz aside. Amy handed Liz a taped-up photograph. "This was in Victoria's trash bin. I taped it back together."

Liz smiled at the image of Victoria in disguise at the dog show. "Perfect."

"There's more." Amy slipped a folded paper into Liz's hand. "Turns out your friend Opal is a bit of an artist. That's a sketch she did for me of the guy I caught nosing around here the other day. It's a good likeness."

Liz unfolded the paper and smiled. "This is fantastic. Thank you."

"It's the same guy?" Amy asked.

"For sure."

Amy glanced at Jackson and headed into the library. Jackson lingered, seemingly reluctant to leave Liz's side. "It's okay," she said. "You go on through to the library too. I'll be fine."

"Are you sure?"

She nodded.

"All right. Be safe." He headed for the library.

She called the chief, who picked up on the first ring. "Did you send Victoria the message?" Liz asked.

"Yup, twenty-five minutes ago. She didn't reply."

"Okay, well, I hope she will after this. We just got to the inn. And you'll be happy to know it was definitely Clive who was here the day my corn knife was stolen. Amy had Opal do a sketch and the resemblance is unmistakable."

"Good. If this doesn't go down as we hope, we're going to need every bit of evidence we can scrounge up to connect him to the attacks on Purcell and Baxter."

"It'll work." Liz hung up and then jogged up the stairs. She knocked on Henry's door. "Henry? It's Liz. If you'd like to come down to the library, I have a surprise for you I think you'll like."

Henry, clothed in only a robe and socks, opened the door a few inches. "Emma?"

Liz grinned.

His expression transformed. "I'll get dressed and be right down," he said, sounding as excited as a kid on Christmas morning.

"Bring Victoria too," Liz said. "I'm sure she'll want to meet her nephew properly."

Henry beamed. "We'll be right there."

As Liz headed downstairs to wait for them, she texted Stan. *The bait's been set.*

Emma was pacing nervously by the time Liz reached the library. "I don't know if I can do this."

"Henry never stopped loving you, Emma. And I doubt he'll ever be able to forgive himself for how much his lack of backbone cost you both. But we can't change the past. You can only move on from here."

Emma blinked back tears, nodding.

Amy smiled at Liz, looking for all the world like a proud mama. She subtly shifted Liz's attention to Jackson, who was gazing at Liz in admiration.

"You're both deeply grieving your son's death," Mary Ann said. "You need each other more than ever. Give your love a second chance."

A moment later Henry appeared at the doorway. "Emma," he said with a depth and warmth that spoke volumes. His eyes glistened with unshed tears.

She froze in the middle of the room. Her grandson, mercifully oblivious to the adult conversation, played with Beans in front of the fireplace.

Henry plunged into the room and clasped Emma's hands, then clutched them to his chest. "I'm so sorry for all the pain I've caused you. The last thing I wanted to do was cause you any more suffering."

She searched his eyes and then freeing a hand from his grasp, cupped his face. "I know, Henry. I know."

Victoria stood in the doorway, frowning at Emma's grandson.

Amy sidled up next to her. "Isn't your brother's son a cutie? How does it feel to suddenly be an auntie?"

Victoria's smile seemed forced. "Surreal." Her hand slipped into her pocket.

Palming her cell phone, Liz hoped.

Victoria looked as if it took every ounce of her self-control to stay put. "Will Emma and her grandson be spending the night here?" Victoria asked.

Liz's skin crawled at the thought of what Victoria might be plotting. "No, I'm afraid I don't have a room for them," Liz said.

Victoria took tentative steps toward her nephew. Patting Beans on the head, she said, "You like dogs, huh?"

"Yeah," Timmy said. "We're learning tricks." He held his hand above Beans's head and said, "High five."

Beans licked the boy's face.

"I don't think he knows that trick," Liz said.

Timmy clasped Beans's paw and showed him what he was supposed to do, then once again held up his hand and said, "High five."

Beans tapped Timmy's hand with his paw.

"Wow, you're a good teacher!" Amy exclaimed.

"Would you like to see another trick?" Victoria asked, reclaiming Timmy's attention.

"What kind?" he asked.

Victoria showed him her empty hands and said, "I can pull money from his ear." She reached behind Beans's floppy ear and produced a shiny quarter, which she handed to Timmy.

His eyes widened.

"Oh, I think you have one too," she said then reached behind Timmy's ear and produced another quarter.

He felt behind his ears for more and came up empty.

Victoria showed him another trick, this time making the quarter seemingly disappear into her elbow.

Liz grew uneasy at how much Timmy was warming up to his aunt . . . and her talent for making people see only what she wanted them to see.

21

"How would everyone like some hot drinks and cookies?" Sadie headed toward the library door, motioning to everyone but Emma and Henry. "You can all help. Let's give these two some privacy."

Victoria's gaze drifted to her father, who was still clasping Emma's hands to his chest and talking animatedly.

"Coming?" Liz asked.

Victoria started after the rest of the group, but hovered outside the door as the others paraded after Sadie.

Jackson paused at Victoria's side, blocking her view of the departing crew. "You look troubled."

She shrugged. "It's a lot to process."

Liz split off from the group and ducked into the sitting room off the opposite side of the foyer. The room was dark, except for a patch of light from the outdoor Christmas lights. There weren't many places to hide in the room—behind the partially closed drapes, behind the sofa, or behind the door. Liz grabbed a wooden puzzle for Timmy from the shelf by the door—her excuse for being here if she were spotted—and slipped behind the sofa.

Jackson's and Victoria's voices sounded closer.

"Do you have a friend you can call? To talk out what you're feeling?" he asked. "That always helps me."

"Yes, that's a good idea," Victoria murmured.

Only Liz wasn't so sure Victoria planned to call her uncle. What if she skipped blasting Clive for not taking care of Timmy and went straight to poisoning Timmy's cocoa?

"Here, use the sitting room," Jackson said, a moment before the overhead light came on. "It'll give you some privacy."

The door creaked, presumably from Jackson closing it for her. Then silence fell over the room for what felt like five minutes, but was probably less than one. The floorboard in front of the window squeaked and Liz shrank back. At the sounds of a cell phone screen being tapped, she dared to breathe again.

"Pick up, pick up," Victoria muttered.

Liz knew the text message the chief sent her earlier from her uncle's phone had simply read: *Everything has been taken care of.*

Liz had hoped Victoria's response would incriminate her. But she was apparently too smart to leave what she had to say in a voice mail. The chief had said Duncan's phone was set to not retain copies of sent messages and his inbox was empty too, presumably because he deleted all messages as soon as he read them. If Victoria took the same precaution, tonight's exchange would be the only solid proof they'd conspired together, unless a cell phone geek could figure out how to recover the deleted messages. Thankfully the chief had found someone who could fake Duncan's voice.

Victoria's phone rang and Liz jumped so hard she almost gave her position away.

"Uncle Clive, what's going on?" Victoria hissed in her phone. "The kid is here at the inn with his grandmother. How's that 'taking care of him?' Do I have to do everything myself?"

Unlike the booming voice mail message, Liz couldn't make out what the impersonator said, even in the silent room.

"Did anyone see you?" Victoria paced.

At the sight of her foot passing the back of the couch, Liz stifled a gasp.

"We're running out of time. Getting rid of the kid won't be enough if Dad manages to woo back Purcell's mother."

To whatever the impersonator said, Victoria snapped, "Leave it to me." She clicked off the phone and stopped pacing.

Liz snuck to the edge of the couch to take a peek.

The woman had pocketed her phone and was studying the contents of a small bottle.

The heart medicine?

Liz's heart turned funky at the prospect. If Victoria was worried about her father remarrying and further fracturing the estate, then chances were good she'd want to take him out of play before he could change his will.

A tap came at the door. "Victoria?" Jackson called and opened the door. "We're serving hot cocoa now."

"Here let me carry that," Victoria said, her voice drifting out of the room.

Liz popped up from behind the couch in time to see Victoria reach for the tray Jackson held. Liz shook her head frantically at Jackson and mouthed *Don't let her.* Victoria must have noticed the shift in his gaze, because she started to turn her head.

Liz dropped behind the couch again, just as Jackson redirected Victoria's attention to the others. Liz waited until she heard their footsteps fade into the library on the other side of the foyer before rising again. She phoned the chief. "You need to get over here. I think she has the poison on her."

"Good, because that conversation gave us enough probable cause to secure a search warrant."

"There's no time. I think she's going to spike the cocoa now. I have to go." Liz clicked off and dashed across the foyer.

Jackson snagged her as she slipped through the door. "Don't worry. I served Victoria last," he whispered in Liz's ear. "She hasn't been close to anyone's drink."

Everyone had gathered on the circle of sofas in the center of the room. Victoria had set her hot cocoa on the coffee table beside her father's.

Liz signaled to Jackson to watch the cups, not sure if they'd already missed any surreptitious tampering. Liz sat down beside Victoria and showed her the picture. "I'm curious why you took this photograph from Sadie's collection only to tear it up and throw it out."

Victoria glanced at the photo. "You searched my room?"

"No," Amy interjected. "Evidence discovered without a warrant wouldn't be admissible in court."

"She's a criminal lawyer," Sadie chimed in.

Victoria blanched, but put on a confused expression. "I don't understand."

"The housekeeper emptied your trash bins when she topped up your linen supply," Amy said.

"If you didn't want the photograph," Sadie said, "you shouldn't have taken it."

Henry leaned over for a look and then cocked his head, his brow furrowing. "Is that you, Victoria?"

"Of course not," she said, scoffing.

"The resemblance is uncanny, isn't it?" Liz said to Henry. "This was taken at the dog show only a few hours before your son was killed."

That got Emma's attention. She snatched the photo from Liz's hand and scrutinized the image.

"How dare you make such innuendoes?" Henry bellowed. "My daughter was in Indianapolis that day."

"You saw her?" Emma asked coolly.

Henry suddenly looked uncertain. His gaze bounced from Emma to the photo to Victoria. "Isn't that what you said?"

"Yes." Victoria lifted her chin. "I was shopping all day."

Henry let out an audible sigh of relief. "There, you see. I'm sure she'll have a few credit card receipts to prove it."

Emma and Liz looked to Victoria for confirmation.

"Actually, I didn't buy anything."

Henry's jaw dropped. Clearly a shopping trip devoid of purchases was not his daughter's usual MO.

Emma poked her finger at the picture and glared at Victoria. "This is you." She turned the photograph to Henry. "Look past the outfit and awful dye and makeup job. That's Victoria. Look at the eyes, the lips, the boots."

Henry's jaw clenched. "This does look a lot like you, Victoria."

"That's ridiculous," Victoria said and nonchalantly took a sip of cocoa. "Why on earth would I come here dressed in a getup like that?"

"To kill Emma's son," Liz said flatly. "Heaven forbid that you should have to share your daddy, let alone his money with your half brother and his child."

Henry's face went white. Emma sprang to her feet, her hands fisted, her jaw tightly clenched.

Mary Ann hurried over to Timmy, who was still in front of the fireplace with Beans, and ensured he wasn't paying attention to this new development.

"Henry hired John Baxter to locate your son," Liz explained quietly to Emma. "I suspect Victoria was here tracking him."

Henry stiffened. "Is this true, Victoria?"

"No!"

"I found another picture of the woman amongst the ones I took," Sadie piped up. She fiddled with her camera in her lap then passed it to Liz. "There in the background on the right. Her back is to the camera, but there's no mistaking the hair and boots."

Liz zoomed in on that section of the photograph. "Yes, and the man she's talking to looks like the same man who paid Rhonda the blackmail ransom for John's tablet. You recognize him?" Liz turned the screen toward Henry.

"That's my brother-in-law, Clive," Henry whispered. He put a noticeable distance between himself and his daughter, giving her a look of horror. "What have you done?"

"Nothing, Father. I swear that's not me." Victoria's expression was the picture of innocence and hurt that her father didn't believe her.

"What the police didn't make public," Liz said to Henry and Emma, "is that the knife wound wasn't what killed your son."

Emma nodded, apparently already aware of that much.

"Both William and John were poisoned with a heart medication," Liz went on. "Didn't your father have a heart condition?" she asked Henry.

"This is ridiculous." Victoria stormed toward the door. "I will not be subjected to any more accusations."

Emma lurched after her, but Liz caught her by the arm at the same time Jackson blocked Victoria's escape.

Victoria's hands slipped into her pockets. "Let me through."

"Why?" Jackson said. "So you can hide the bottle before you're caught with it on you?"

"No!" Emma whirled toward her grandson and knocked the mug of hot cocoa flying out of his grip. It crashed against the hearth, spilling cocoa everywhere.

Timmy burst into tears. "Grandma, why did you do that?"

Emma soothed him. "The drink was bad, sweetheart. Grandma didn't want you to get sick. Did you drink any?"

"He didn't," Mary Ann assured her, hauling Beans away from the spilled cocoa. "I'd just brought it over to him."

Henry yanked his daughter's hands out of her pants pockets. They came out empty. He patted her down and a moment later, pulled a small vial from her jacket pocket. "What are you doing with your grandfather's medicine?" he demanded.

Victoria shrugged. "It must've been in my pocket from the last time I took care of him. I don't wear this jacket often."

She's a cool customer.

Emma was on her knees in front of her grandson, cradling his head to her chest. She covered his ear with her palm and said, "Call the police."

"They're already on their way," Liz said.

Victoria's gaze flared.

"I heard your little conversation with your uncle," Liz said. "Only it wasn't your uncle on the other end of the line. He was arrested hours ago for assault and attempted kidnapping."

The woman finally looked scared. Her hands visibly shook. "Daddy," she wheedled. "It's not what you think. I told Uncle Clive what you were doing. I was upset. All I could think about was what people would start saying about Mom once the news got out."

The anguish on Henry's face made Liz's heart ache for him.

"I swear I had no idea what he had planned," Victoria went on.

"The waitress and the bartender both placed you, not your uncle, at the bar the afternoon John met William there," Liz said.

"You killed my son? Your brother?" Henry said, sounding as if his heart was being ripped from his chest.

Emma, looking equally anguished, opened her mouth, but whatever she'd been about to say was eclipsed by Victoria's explosive reaction.

"My son. My son. *My son.* That's all you've talked about for months." Victoria's furious gaze burned into him. "You have a daughter too, you know."

The swirl of police lights danced across the library's windows as two cruisers pulled up to the inn.

"Please, Daddy," Victoria pleaded, her tone abruptly changing.

"You have to believe me. I didn't want—"

"You killed my son."

The police chief pushed past Jackson into the room. "Not quite, but she gave it a good effort."

"What?" everyone exclaimed.

Emma released her grandson and stood, a sheepish smile tugging on her lips.

Officer Gerst wheeled a man in a wheelchair into the room.

"Daddy!" Timmy squealed and ran to the man, arms wide.

The man scooped him up onto his lap and hugged him tight.

"You're William?" Liz said, dumbfounded. The same William she'd seen in a body bag?

"Call me Bill." He grinned over his son's head at his mother.

All eyes turned to Emma, who was also smiling broadly, not looking the least bit surprised. "You knew?" Liz asked.

Emma ducked her head. "I'm sorry. The chief convinced me to go along with Bill's plan. I didn't like deceiving you."

Bill. Liz turned back to him. "You're the one who called John's phone when the Amish boy answered?"

He nodded.

"He's worse about taking orders than you are, Liz," the chief muttered.

Emma reached out to Henry and clasped his arm. "I especially hated to cause you so much pain." She tugged him toward Bill. "Let me introduce you to our son."

Behind him, Officer Gerst arrested a gaping Victoria, cuffing her hands.

"How can this be?" Liz asked the chief. "We saw him in the body bag. You said the reason he didn't bleed out from the knife stab was because he was already dead."

"Trust me. We thought he was dead when we put him in that body bag. But when the medical examiner opened the body bag, William was alive. It happens from time to time."

"What about the stab wound?" Jackson asked.

"Superficial."

"And why did you let everyone think he was dead?" Liz said.

Stan gave her a pained look, betraying his true feelings about the ruse.

Liz recalled a similar pained look when he'd asked Mary Ann not to encourage Liz to investigate John's disappearance. She immediately realized he'd been trying to protect her.

"I didn't actually say he was dead in the media release the next morning," the chief said in his defense. "Everyone inferred it, because the reporter on the scene the night before had already run the story. When Bill came to and learned that John was missing, he assumed John had poisoned his drink, probably paid off by someone who didn't want Henry to find him, or maybe Henry himself. Since we didn't know for sure who had tried to kill him, it was best that as few people as possible knew he was still alive."

"So you figured letting everyone believe he was dead would make it easier to flush out his killer?"

"It was Bill's idea," Stan said. His gaze became stern. "If you recall, I asked you to stay out of it more than once."

"Yeah, I did think that wasn't like you."

"Did the scare at the cabin convince you to hang up your deerstalker?"

Liz smiled at the sight of Henry hugging his son and grandson as Emma looked on. "Nope, I don't think so."

From the other side of the room, Jackson added, "Some things are worth the risk."

Their gazes collided and something about the gleam in Jackson's eye made Liz think he might have been referring to a different kind of risk.

22

Two days before Christmas, Amy's squeal brought Liz running. Beans uncharacteristically raced ahead of her to the foyer.

Ever since Peanut's brief visit at the beginning of the month, or maybe it was falling for the border collie at the dog show, or winning the best costume award, Beans seemed eager to inspect every new arrival. And apparently a guest special enough to draw a squeal from Amy was worth expending an extra burst of energy.

Liz headed for the foyer to find Amy holding a giant cellophane-wrapped basket of chocolates and Christmas ornaments and who knew what else, beaming up at John Baxter, who was sporting a pair of crutches and a cast on one leg. John leaned down and planted a kiss on the top of Amy's head.

Whoa. Amy's visits to John in the hospital had clearly been friendlier than Liz had realized.

"John, it's great to see you up and about."

He grinned at her even as color tinged his cheeks. "Yup, thanks to you and Amy."

Amy handed Liz the gift basket.

"It's lovely," Liz said, inviting them into the sitting room. "Thank you."

John sat down awkwardly on the sofa, leaning his crutches against the arm. Beans waddled up beside him, and John leaned over to scratch his back. The bulldog rewarded John with a sloppy kiss. Amy dropped down beside him and John clasped her hand.

"I wish I could take credit," Amy said. "But the basket is from Henry and Emma. They asked me to bring it when they heard I was coming back."

Liz sat down and opened the card that waxed on about their appreciation for all she'd done. "How are they doing?" Liz asked John.

"They're great. William has fully recovered and, in the interest of sparing his father further distress, he's magnanimously asked the prosecutor to cut his half sister and Clive a much better deal than they deserve."

"Given the defense team the pair acquired," Amy added. "The deal would also save all of them years of ongoing litigation."

"I sincerely hope Victoria can let go of her resentment toward her father and embrace the second chance at a family she's been given. And I hope Henry and Emma can forgive her." Liz began to unwrap her gift.

"Time will tell," John said and then looked deep into Amy's eyes. "I've sure learned to cherish every moment. You never know which one might be your last."

"Stop that," Amy said, giving his arm a playful swat. "Your last moment—and mine—won't be for a long, long time."

Liz's heart swelled at the joy in her friend's face. Could it be? "You mean—?"

Amy laughed. "All the tests came back negative. Well, not *all* the tests. I need to monitor my blood sugar, which means no more visits to Naomi's bakery. But that's a small—if painful—price to pay for a new lease on life."

Liz jumped up at the same time Amy did and embraced her friend. "So you'll be asking for your old job back at the law firm? Going back to Boston?"

Amy glanced over at John, who beamed back at her. "Nope. My adventure with you has given me a taste for investigating. John's asked me to help out at his PI firm for a while. If I like the work, I can start the process of getting my investigator's license."

Liz couldn't help but wonder if another kind of license might be in Amy and John's future. She sincerely hoped that this was how Amy would always be: happy, laughing, and full of life.

And, like Liz, sharing the season with people she loved.

Learn more about Annie's fiction books at

AnniesFiction.com

We've designed the Annie's Fiction website especially for you!

Access your e-books · Read sample chapters · Manage your account

Choose from one of these great series:

Amish Inn Mysteries

Annie's Attic Mysteries

Annie's Mysteries Unraveled

Annie's Quilted Mysteries

Annie's Secrets of the Quilt

Antique Shop Mysteries

Chocolate Shoppe Mysteries

Creative Woman Mysteries

Hearts of Amish Country

Secrets of the Castleton Manor Library

Victorian Mansion Flower Shop Mysteries

What are you waiting for? Visit us now at **AnniesFiction.com!**